W9-CBS-641

Dear Reader:

We asked our editors to find us something really special as a holiday gift for our Reader Service members and they have created this volume just for you.

It's our Christmas present to you, a small token of appreciation for being a loyal reader and for allowing us into your life...and into your heart.

We hope you will enjoy Christy and Matt's story and we hope you have a happy, glowing holiday season.

Candy Lee

UNDER THE
MISTLETOE

by Tracy Sinclair

Harlequin Books®

ISBN: 0-373-15138-1

UNDER THE MISTLETOE
Copyright © 1986 by Tracy Sinclair
Originally published in
Silhouette Christmas Stories
Copyright © 1986 by Silhouette Books

Printed in the U.S.A.

Chapter One

I'm not sure we made enough sandwiches," Sarah Blake remarked to her niece as she surveyed the buffet table with a critical eye.

There seemed to be plenty of everything. In addition to large platters of sandwiches, there were bowls of nuts and potato chips, trays of cookies and several layer cakes.

Christy Blake looked fondly at the older woman. This annual open house had been a Christmas Eve tradition ever since she'd come to live at Sky Ranch with her aunt. Invitations were by word of mouth, so they never knew how many to expect. Anyone lonely or down on his luck was welcome, along with friends and neighbors.

There had been dire warnings about the dangers of two women alone taking strangers into the house, but Sarah Blake had been trusting her own instincts for fifty-eight years. So far, they hadn't failed her.

"We've never run out of sandwiches yet, but if we do I'll make some more," Christy promised.

"Half the party would follow you into the kitchen," Sarah answered dryly, gazing at her niece's flowerlike face.

Christy had been an adorable teenager when she had come to live with her father's only sister after being orphaned tragically. She was blessed with delicate features, silky blond hair and thickly lashed blue eyes.

When her adolescent body matured into a curved figure and long slim legs, Christy was breathtaking. No one could understand why someone that outstanding remained in a little town like Pine Grove, which was only a village nestled in the northern California mountains.

"Here they come," Sarah announced as the doorbell rang.

People arrived regularly from then on. Christy divided her time between answering the door and circulating among the guests, making the ones who didn't know anybody feel at ease. The rooms were soon crowded with smiling people filled with the holiday spirit.

Matt Destry's handsome face didn't reflect the joyousness of the season. He was scowling at the twisting mountain road beyond the windshield of his sleek Jaguar sports coupe. The snow that was coming down like a lacy white curtain made visibility poor. The ski resort at Squaw Valley, where he was headed, was normally a four hour drive from San Francisco, but at this rate there was no telling how long it would take.

Matt's scowl could have been due to concentration, but it wasn't. He was feeling sorry for himself, all alone on Christmas Eve. The fact that he had turned down invitations to several parties didn't console him. And the knowledge that it would never occur to anyone else to feel sorry for him merely irritated Matt. He knew how the world perceived him—as the man who had it all.

The electronics company he'd started in a garage was now one of the largest in the industry. At thirty-three he was already a millionaire, with all the appropriate trappings of success: the penthouse apartment with a view that included the Golden Gate Bridge; lavish offices occupying a whole floor of the Transamerica Building; his suits were custom-made by an expensive tailor; he belonged to the best clubs and his girlfriends were always the most glamorous at any gathering.

So why did he feel subtly discontented lately? Perhaps because everyone he encountered seemed to want something from him, both men and women. Was it unrealistic to expect to be liked for himself alone? As soon as people found out he was president of CompuTrend, they had a whole wish list for Matt to fulfill.

Blinding headlights in the rearview mirror put an end to his somber thoughts temporarily. A pickup truck had appeared out of nowhere, traveling at a rate of speed that would be unsafe on a sunny summer day. Such speed was practically suicidal at night in a snowstorm.

Matt could scarcely believe it when the truck swung out to pass him as they were approaching a blind curve. When the truck drew abreast the radio was blaring loud enough for him to hear it through his closed window. After that, everything happened so swiftly that Matt acted out of instinct.

A car rounded the curve ahead, on a direct collision course with the truck. Matt swung sharply to the right to give the pickup room to get back in the proper lane. The Jaguar went into a skid, and he fought to keep it under control as he steered between giant pine trees laden with snow. There was a hideous grating sound as hidden rocks scraped the low undercarriage before the sports car came to a shuddering stop.

For a long moment Matt sat motionless behind the wheel. Then he started to swear savagely. That truck full of drunks could have killed everyone in all three vehicles! He got out of the car, flexing his tense muscles.

The intense cold immediately penetrated his light clothing. Since he hadn't expected to stop anywhere along the way, Matt had worn jeans, a T-shirt and a light denim jacket. It was too cold to stand by the roadside hoping someone would come along and give him a lift to the nearest town. No one would stop to investigate the wreck either, since the Jaguar was hidden from sight by a clump of trees. His only hope was finding a house out here in this godforsaken wilderness. Matt's generous mouth was compressed in a grim line as he wrapped his arms around his lean body and started slogging through the deep snow.

He was shivering so badly that his teeth were chattering by the time he finally found a lighted house. The sign over the arched front gate said Sky Ranch. Through the windows Matt could see that a party was in progress. Laughter mingled with the sweet sound of Christmas carols playing on a stereo set.

"Bah, humbug!" he muttered as he pressed the bell.

Christy opened the door with her usual welcoming smile. It changed to a startled awareness as she gazed at the newcomer. Her senses registered everything about him in one lightning instant: his powerful, lean-limbed body; his dark blue, intelligent eyes that seemed a little jaded; his straight nose and well-formed mouth. It even crossed her mind to wonder where he got such a deep tan in the middle of winter.

Matt was forming his own surprised impressions. He was used to beautiful women, but there was something about Christy that set her apart from the ones he knew. It wasn't only her beauty, although she was the most exquisite girl Matt had ever seen. Perhaps it was the air of innocence she radiated, he decided as he stared down into her wide, lovely eyes. She was like a slender, unawakened fawn, arousing a protectiveness Matt hadn't felt in years. It was neither required, nor desired by the women of his acquaintance.

Christy recovered first. She pinned her conventional smile back in place. "Please come in. We're so glad you could join us."

Matt looked surprised. "I don't want to interrupt your party, but—"

"There's plenty of food," she assured him before he could continue. "Just take a plate and help yourself."

"You don't understand. I was on my way to Squaw Valley, and—"

"Don't worry, we're very casual here," Christy interrupted again, acknowledging his jeans and T-shirt. She knew what was bothering him, and her soft heart melted. The poor man didn't have any decent clothes.

"Are you trying to freeze us out?" Sarah appeared at the door. "Come inside, young man, before we all catch pneumonia." She took his arm and led him to the buffet table. "I hope you like turkey, because we're all out of ham. My name's Sarah Blake, and I assume you met my niece, Christy."

Matt supplied his own name automatically before saying, "This is very kind of you, but I just came to use the telephone."

She looked at him shrewdly. So this was one of the ones who was ashamed of being hard up. "As long as you're here, why don't you have a sandwich first?" she asked casually. "Christy always makes too many, and if you don't help us out we'll be stuck with them. A big fellow like you doesn't have to be hungry to put away a little snack."

"Actually, I'm starving," Matt admitted. He had expected to have a late dinner at the hotel.

"Dig in then. And when you're finished, the telephone is in the hall," she added, to help him save face.

Matt felt a little better after he had eaten and thawed out. He was confused, though. What kind of people invited a perfect stranger into the house? When some of the other guests told him about Sarah's Christmas Eve tradition, he was even more baffled. Matt was used to the paranoia of the city. People there didn't even invite their neighbors in!

A frown creased his forehead as he watched Christy's graceful figure moving around the room. If the older woman didn't have sense enough to worry about her own safety, she ought to be concerned about her niece's. That beautiful girl shouldn't be exposed to danger.

Matt's own troubles occupied his full attention a short time later. When he finally got through to the auto club, a dispatcher told him they couldn't tow his car. There were calls stacked up that would take all night. To make matters worse, they were going to be closed on Christmas Day.

"What the hell is someone supposed to do if his car breaks down?" Matt's indignation crackled across the telephone wire.

"Don't ask me, Mac, I only work here." The line went dead with a note of finality.

So much for goodwill toward men, Matt thought grimly. Now what? Where was he going to find a hotel on the side of a mountain? Even if one existed it would have to be nearby, because he couldn't wander very far dressed as he was. Sleeping in the car was out, too. He'd freeze to death by morning.

Sarah paused on her way through the hall, looking disapprovingly at Matt's ferocious scowl. "Christmas is a time for rejoicing, young man. Instead of dwelling on your troubles, try counting your blessings."

Matt's mouth curved sardonically. "I'd be happy to if one of them was a hotel room."

"You don't have anyplace to sleep?"

"Not tonight, although I do have expectations for the future—if I have one," he added wryly.

Sarah stared at him speculatively as she made up her mind. "In that case, you can stay here tonight."

"You must be joking!" Incredulity was written all over Matt's face. "I could be a murderer or a rapist for all you know."

"Are you?"

"No, of course not!"

"Then there's no problem. I'll have Christy show you the guest room after the party." As Matt's expression changed unconsciously, Sarah said, "Make no mistake, young man, the invitation does not include my niece. If you have any ideas about wandering around during the night, you'll find neither of us is a helpless weakling."

"I would never make that mistake about you, at any rate." Matt looked at his hostess with respect.

"Don't underestimate Christy, either. There's more to that girl than a pretty face. Now go mingle with the guests. Enjoy yourself," Sarah ordered.

Matt followed her into the living room, but he found a corner where he could watch the festivities unobtrusively. He still had a dazed feeling of unreality about this whole night. Especially when Christy came over to join him. She was almost too perfect to be real.

Christy's smile expressed more confidence than she felt. There was something very daunting about this man. He looked as though he lived hard and played hard. His taut body had the power and grace of a jungle cat. If he wanted something badly enough, he would take it—including a woman.

With a flash of perception, Christy knew he would never have to use force. Women would share his bed willingly, and he would bring them pleasure beyond their wildest dreams. A tingling sensation raced through her veins as she imagined that lean, hawklike face poised over hers in the velvet darkness.

Christy's ivory skin warmed with color at the unbidden thought. It was so totally unlike her! "Aunt Sarah tells me you're staying here tonight," she said brightly.

"I hope you don't mind."

"Not at all."

Matt hesitated. "Does she do this sort of thing often? Ask strange men to stay the night, I mean."

Christy looked at him curiously. "Actually, you're the first one. You already know about these annual Christmas Eve parties, and there are all kinds of other causes she's interested in, but she's never taken anyone into the house before."

"Well, thank God for that!"

"Why?"

"*Why?* Because it could be dangerous. Take me, for instance. You don't know anything about me."

"I know you need a helping hand," Christy said simply.

Matt's eyes darkened to navy as he stared down at her upturned face. "You're very sweet, Christy, but I don't want to mislead you. I'm not broke and hungry as you suppose." When her eyes slid away from his, Matt remembered how he had wolfed down the sandwiches. "Well, I'll admit I was hungry when I arrived, but that was only because—"

"You don't have to explain," she interposed gently. "Anyone can have a run of bad luck."

He ruffled his thick dark hair in frustration. "How can I convince you?"

"Why does it matter?"

He examined her lovely features with a sense of wonderment. "I don't know, but it does. For the first time in my life, I want to brag about being at the top of the heap. I want to tell you everything I've done, and all the the things I hope to do in the future."

"You will, Matt." Her voice was very soft. "Aunt Sarah saw something special in you, and I do, too. I know you'll succeed eventually. We both have faith in you."

"It doesn't matter that I didn't even have a place to stay tonight?" he demanded.

Christy smiled. "You aren't the first person to look for lodgings on Christmas Eve." She saw her aunt beckoning. "I think Aunt Sarah wants us to mingle. If you know what's good for you, you'll do it."

Matt's intense expression changed to a broad grin. "I already got that impression. It was right after she told me you were off-limits."

Christy frowned. "That doesn't sound like Aunt Sarah. She's always trusted me to use my own judgment."

"Maybe I'm the one she doesn't trust." Matt's husky voice was very sensuous.

As their eyes met, something electric seemed to leap between them. He didn't touch her, but Christy got the impression that he was making love to her. It was almost as though she could feel his firm mouth moving over hers in an exquisite prelude. She wanted to move into his arms and let him mold her body to his hard contours.

Matt was the one who broke the spell. "Your aunt is a very wise woman," he said, smiling ruefully.

Christy was confused and troubled by her incomprehensible reaction to this man. It wasn't as though she hadn't had more than her share of male attention. She wasn't an impressionable teenager. Admittedly, Matt was an awesome specimen of masculinity, but she had met handsome men before.

What was this strange hold Matt Destry had over her? He was a homeless drifter who had appeared out of nowhere, and would disappear just as anonymously. She didn't know any more about him than that. He had even issued a subtle warning not to trust him. But strangely enough, Christy did. It was herself she was uncertain about.

The last guests didn't leave until almost midnight. When Matt looked at his watch, he was amazed to see how the time had flown. Usually he was restless at parties, bored by the empty chatter and ready to leave almost as soon as he arrived. But this evening he really enjoyed talking to the local residents. It delighted Matt to have people listen to him because he had something to say, not because he was Matt Destry, president of CompuTrend Industries.

Sarah surveyed the littered rooms after everyone had left. "Well, if debris means anything, I think everybody had a good time."

"That shouldn't come as any surprise." Christy began gathering used glasses and plates. "They always do."

"Just carry those things into the kitchen and leave them," her aunt instructed. "You'll be late for midnight service."

Christy slanted a glance at Matt. "Maybe I won't bother this year."

"You've been looking forward to it all day." Sarah correctly interpreted her reluctance. "Take Matt with you. A little sermon might do him good."

His eyes danced with laughter. "I always heard there was no free lunch."

"You don't have to go," Christy said hastily.

"I'd consider it an honor." There was a little catch in his voice as he gazed into her clear blue eyes. "It would be the perfect ending to a wonderful evening."

Christy looked suddenly doubtful. "You aren't dressed very warmly, and the heater in my car is broken."

"Take the pickup," Sarah suggested. She sized up Matt's tall, rangy frame. "And get Matt that old sheepskin coat Jake Dingle left behind when he quit. It'll keep him warm, even if it is a little skimpy."

They were ready to leave when Sarah noticed that Christy was still wearing the shoes that matched the silver belt on her white silk dress.

"You can't go out in this weather with those flimsy little sandals. Where are your boots?" she demanded.

"They won't fit over high heels," Christy explained.

"Then change to sensible shoes."

"There isn't time. I want Matt to hear the Christmas carols. Besides, the truck is in the garage. We'll go through the kitchen door."

"How about when you get to—" Sarah's protest was addressed to empty air. She listened to their hasty sounds of departure for a long moment. "I hope my instincts didn't pick this one time to be wrong," she muttered with a slight frown.

It had stopped snowing. The full moon shone down on a fairy-tale landscape painted in black and white. The tall pines were decorated with puffs of snow that reflected the sparkle of the glittering stars overhead. They formed a border around fields completely carpeted in white.

"I love it when it's quiet like this," Christy exclaimed. "Isn't it beautiful?"

Matt was gazing at the pure line of her profile as she watched the narrow road ahead. "I've never seen anything so lovely," he said in a muted voice.

"I hope you'll like the service," she remarked self-consciously. "I think it will be something different for you anyway, although I don't know what you're used to."

Matt never knew why he didn't tell her the truth right then. Afterward, he decided it was because he didn't want to shatter the dream. For this one night he wanted to be anonymous, free to be a man instead of a myth.

"I'm used to all sorts of things." He smiled. "I'm very adaptable."

"I suppose you've had to be."

She slanted a sideways glance at him. The faint light from the dashboard shaded Matt's high cheekbones and turned his eyes to inscrutable navy pools. The shifting shadows gave his face a predatory look.

"I can't complain." He shrugged off her sympathy.

"What kind of work do you usually do?" Christy asked delicately.

Matt chuckled. "You want to know what kind of work I'm out of?"

"I didn't mean to—"

"It's all right, honey." His big hand covered her slim fingers on the steering wheel. "I'm an engineer."

Christy was startled, although there was something about Matt that set him apart from the ordinary. "Surely you could get a job in your field."

"There isn't much hiring done at holiday time." That was true, he told himself.

"Well, don't worry, I'm sure things will get busy after the first of the year."

Matt sighed. "I suppose so."

"You mustn't get discouraged," she said earnestly. "A lot of people are in your predicament. You'll pull yourself out of it, though."

"Is that the standard pep talk you give to all of Aunt Sarah's lame ducks?" Matt asked dryly.

"Only when it's the truth," she assured him. "People can always tell when you're lying, and then they don't trust you. I really do believe you'll make a success of your life."

Matt was beginning to feel uncomfortable, but it would have been a little awkward to confess all at that particular moment. "The party's over and you've played the encouraging hostess long enough," he said lightly. "Tell me something about yourself. Have you lived here long?"

"Yes. I came to stay with Aunt Sarah when I was fifteen, after my parents were killed in a car crash. She's as dear to me as my own mother."

"I didn't meet her husband," Matt suddenly recalled. "Is your aunt a widow?"

Christy shook her head. "She never married. There was a fiancé once who was killed in the war. He was the great love of her life. It's sad that no one could ever take his place, but she's made a full life for herself in Pine Grove.''

"It's rather a small town," Matt observed tentatively.

Christy sighed unconsciously. "Not to Aunt Sarah. She's completely happy right here."

"How about you?"

"I'm happy too." Christy's voice was slightly defensive. "She's been wonderful to me."

"What do you do? What kind of work, I mean."

"There aren't many jobs in Pine Grove, so I commute to Squaw Valley. It's about an hour's drive. I work for a realtor."

"You sell real estate?"

"No, I just work in the office—doing paper work mostly." She sounded vaguely discontented.

"One of life's necessary evils," Matt commented.

"I suppose so."

"What would you prefer doing?"

"All kinds of things! I got interested in the theater when I took drama in college. It's fascinating what you can do with a small stage. I'd love to get into set design, or maybe lighting." Her face sparkled with animation.

"Not acting?"

"I prefer the production end." The sparkle died. "It's just wishful thinking, though. There isn't even a little theater here."

"San Francisco isn't far away."

"I couldn't leave Aunt Sarah."

"She doesn't seem like the helpless sort." Matt chuckled. "Much less a clinging vine."

"Far from it! She's urged me to strike out on my own, but I'd worry about her terribly, all alone on the ranch."

"You intend to stay here the rest of your life?"

Christy's mouth curved in a lopsided smile. "It looks that way. I can't even get Aunt Sarah to take a trip with me."

Before Matt could reply, they arrived at the church, a small white building with a tall spire. Lights streaming out of the windows painted a golden circle in the snow. The voices of people greeting one another as they walked up the path mingled with Christmas carols coming from the church. It was the kind of charming, old-fashioned scene that Matt hadn't known still existed.

The early arrivals had taken the parking spaces near the entrance, so Christy was forced to park a short distance away. She looked dubiously from her open sandals to the deep snow on the ground. While she was bracing herself to take the plunge, Matt came around to the driver's side.

He scooped her into his arms, smiling down at her. "Now you know what Aunt Sarah was trying to tell you."

Christy was acutely conscious of the close contact with his lean body. The arm she put around his shoulders rested on solid muscle, and she could feel the tautness of his broad chest, even cushioned by her heavy coat and Matt's sheepskin jacket. He was rather dauntingly masculine.

"I suppose I should have listened to her," she said breathlessly.

His navy eyes had pinpoints of light as he gazed down at the golden hair spilling over his shoulder. "I'm glad you didn't," he murmured.

Christy's breath caught in her throat as she stared into the dark face so close to her own. The tiny laugh she managed sounded forced. "I'll bet you didn't know what you were letting yourself in for when you rang our bell tonight."

His teeth gleamed whitely. "Never in my wildest dreams."

"You didn't have to come with me," she said doubtfully.

Matt's laughter died. "I'll never forget this night as long as I live," he answered softly.

Christy was both relieved and reluctant when he put her down in the entry of the church. The emotions this enigmatic man aroused were very confusing. She didn't relax until the service began.

The pastor's sermon was on love and trust. It engrossed Christy so much that she wasn't aware of Matt's eyes resting often on her face. His expression would have surprised both of them.

At the end of the service, candles were passed out. The church lights were turned off and the whole congregation joined in singing "Silent Night." The lovely music sounded even more moving in the flickering candlelight. As the last pure notes died away, the lights came on and everyone turned to greet his neighbor and shake hands.

When Christy and Matt turned back to each other, he took both her hands. "Merry Christmas, little Christy," he said. "May all of your wishes come true."

"And yours, too," she whispered.

They stared into each other's eyes with a kind of wonder. It was as though something very special was about to happen. The magic moment slipped by when friends came over to say hello.

As they made their way toward the exit, Christy held out the car keys. "Would you mind bringing the truck around?"

Matt laughed. "Wasn't my door-to-door service satisfactory?"

"Well, uh, this way is easier."

"But not as much fun," he teased, his eyes glinting with mischief. "Okay, honey, if that's what you want."

Christy watched as he moved away lithely, remembering the feeling of being in his arms. It wouldn't be prudent to repeat the experience. Although Matt had been a perfect gentleman so far, she sensed that his expertise with women was awesome. Without even touching her, he had aroused emotions that made her heart beat like a tom-tom.

Christy liked the competent way Matt negotiated the icy roads. She had complete confidence in him as she studied his strong profile while they discussed the service.

"The candlelight ceremony was very moving," he remarked.

"It's a tradition that everyone looks forward to. People come from miles around to take part."

"I don't wonder. It was every bit as impressive in its way as the services at St. Paul's in London."

Christy's eyebrows rose. "Have you been there?"

A slight frown creased Matt's broad forehead. "Everybody's heard of them. Do I turn left here?" he asked before she could comment.

When they returned home the kitchen was neat, and Sarah had gone to bed.

"Would you like a cup of hot chocolate?" Christy asked. She was reluctant to see the evening end.

"Not really—unless you would," Matt said politely.

"No, I . . . I just thought it might help you get to sleep."

"I don't think I'll have any trouble." He laughed. "It's been quite a day."

"Yes, well, I'll show you to your room." She hesitated in the doorway. The quiet room seemed suddenly intimate, making her self-conscious.

Matt's expression changed as he looked at her slender figure. The white silk dress outlined Christy's high, firm breasts and clung to her tiny waist before falling in soft folds.

He moved toward her with the lithe grace of a panther. Before she knew what to expect, he put his arms around her waist.

"What are you doing?" she gasped.

Matt tilted his chin to look up at the mistletoe hanging overhead. "This is a Christmas tradition, too." He bent his head toward hers, but when Christy stiffened, he paused. "Just one kiss?"

Her panic subsided. Christy knew if she said no, he would let her go. Her rigid body relaxed, and she raised her face.

As Matt's firm lips touched hers, his arms tightened, drawing her slim body closer. His hands moved over her back in a sensuous rhythm that made tiny flames leap in Christy's veins. She felt herself turning liquid inside as his mouth devoured hers and his long fingers combed through her silky hair.

"Sweet, adorable Christy," he murmured. "You're like a beautiful dream. I've never met anyone so perfect."

His husky voice was smoky with desire, fanning the flames. Christy sensed that she was out of her depth. This man had experience beyond her knowledge. "You've known a lot of women, haven't you?" she whispered.

He touched the petal softness of her cheek almost reverently. "But none like you. I don't even understand the way I feel about you."

"Am I so different?" she asked uncertainly.

He cradled her head on his shoulder and buried his face in the shining brightness of her hair. "Partly because you don't even know why. Don't ever change, sweetheart."

Matt's hard body was awakening needs Christy hadn't been aware of. She moved unconsciously against him. His arms tightened for a moment before he put her firmly away.

"I think it's time you pointed the way to my room—*now!*" he stated.

Christy led the way down the hall silently. He was wise to call a halt. She should have done it herself, but when she was in Matt's arms it had seemed so right. She turned to leave with a murmured good-night, but he caught her hand.

"Thank you for the most memorable night of my life." He raised her hand and kissed the palm. "Merry Christmas, honey," Matt said gently.

Chapter Two

It was a long time before Christy got to sleep that night. She tried to put Matt out of her mind. He was a drifter. After tomorrow she would never see him again. He might even be gone before she got up. That thought made her even more tense.

Christy overslept the next morning after her brief, restless night. There were sounds coming from the kitchen, which meant Aunt Sarah was already making breakfast. When she didn't hear Matt's deep voice, Christy scrambled out of bed and ran down the hall without bothering to put on a robe. She stopped abruptly on seeing Matt alone in the kitchen.

"I thought maybe you'd gone," she said breathlessly.

"Without saying goodbye? That wouldn't be polite." He smiled as he gazed at her tousled hair and sleepy face. "Besides, your aunt asked me to stay for Christmas dinner."

Christy brightened considerably. That meant he would be there another whole day! "Where is Aunt Sarah?"

"She isn't back from church yet, so I started breakfast. How do you like your eggs?"

"You didn't have to do that," she protested. "I'll make breakfast."

"Don't you think you should put on some slippers first?" He looked appreciatively at her long bare legs exposed by the short flannel gown.

"Oh!" Until then Christy wasn't aware of how she was dressed. "I'll be right back."

"Take your time. Everything's under control."

After a quick shower, Christy put on jeans and a red-and-white checked shirt. The ranch hands had Christmas off, but the chores still had to be done. She tied her long hair back with a ribbon and hurried to the kitchen. Sarah had returned by then and breakfast was ready.

"You're a handy man to have around," Sarah said approvingly as she bit into a slice of perfectly browned bacon. "Have you had restaurant experience?"

Matt grinned. "No, but I've had to cook for myself, and I'm a harsh critic."

"You might give it some thought as a career," she remarked.

"Matt is an engineer," Christy said.

"A professional man! I knew there was something about you," Sarah exclaimed triumphantly. "I get so impatient with people who keep telling me not to trust strangers—as though I couldn't spot a phony when I saw one. My instincts haven't been wrong yet!"

"People may be right," Matt said quietly. "There's always a first time."

"Nonsense! Tell me about yourself. Are you hoping to build bridges and things?"

"No, I, uh, I'm interested in electronics."

Sarah nodded understandingly. "I hear there's been a recession in that field, but I'm sure things will ease up and you'll find a job."

Matt heartily cursed the whim that had made him go along with the charade of being unemployed. He couldn't continue to accept their hospitality under false pretenses. "I'm afraid I gave you the wrong impression last night. I'm not what you think I am."

"You don't have to explain to us," Sarah said firmly. "It isn't any disgrace to be down on your luck, Matt. We like you for what you are, not what you have. The important thing is that you're a genuine, honest human being."

"And when you're a big success you can write and tell us about it," Christy said softly.

He looked from one to the other, unable to say a word.

After breakfast Sarah said, "I'd better get the turkey in the oven before people begin stopping by. And you have to start on the chores," she told Christy.

"I'll help," Matt offered.

The snow had stopped, and the sun was a bright circle in the clear blue sky. Fresh snow glittered in the sunlight like miles of crushed diamonds. Only bird and rabbit tracks marred the smooth surface. It was clear, but very cold, and Christy was shivering before they even got to the hen house.

They had just finished feeding the chickens when there was a loud whinny outside. Christy frowned. "All the horses are supposed to be in the stable or the exercise yard."

They were greeted at the door by a magnificent palomino stallion. He tossed his head and swished his blond tail when he saw them, as though in triumph at his cleverness.

"Oh, no! It's Mischief," Christy groaned. "He's gotten out of the corral again."

"I gather by his name that he's done this before," Matt remarked.

"He should have been named Houdini," she grumbled. "Now I'll have to fix the fence."

"No problem. Show me where it is and I'll do it."

While Matt repaired the torn fencing, Christy chased Mischief back to the stable. It was no easy task. He was enjoying the romp, even if she wasn't. By the time she finally prevailed, and Matt finished with the fence, they were both thoroughly chilled.

"Let's go in the barn and warm up," Christy suggested.

It felt almost balmy inside after the sharp cold. They sat on a bed of sweet smelling hay while Christy removed her boots and shook out the snow.

"Blast that animal!" she said disgustedly. "He's always up to something. I wish there was a juvenile delinquent home for horses."

"He only wanted a little freedom." Matt's face was enigmatic. "Haven't you ever had that feeling?"

Christy slanted a startled look at him, then concentrated on her boots. "He has a good home, gentle treatment and plenty to eat. What more could a horse want?"

"That's enough for an animal," Matt agreed. "People are a different story. There's a whole world out there, Christy."

She didn't look up. "I thought we were talking about horses."

He stared at her bent head for a long moment. "That's true." He sighed. "I have no right to try to impose my values on you. They haven't even made me that happy."

She looked up then, troubled. "You will be, Matt. Someday all of your dreams will come true."

He made a sound of exasperation. "Why are you always concerned about other people? How about *your* dreams?"

"Maybe they'll come true too." A dimple appeared enchantingly at the corner of her mouth. "I'm working on it."

"How?"

"Promise you won't laugh?" When she received assurance, Christy said, "I've always wanted to travel to far-off places and do exciting things. You know, like snorkeling in Bermuda and skiing the Bavarian Alps." Her face was dreamy.

"Those places aren't so distant these days."

"They are for me." She sighed.

Matt frowned at the wistfulness in her eyes. "Are you waiting for your fairy godmother to make an airplane out of a pumpkin? *Do* something about it!"

"I told you, I am." She laughed self-consciously. "You've seen those contests where the grand prize is an all expense paid trip to somewhere glamorous? I enter every one I can find."

"You're kidding!"

"Well, someone has to win," she said defensively. "The only trouble is, I've sent in so many entry forms that if I ever do win, I won't remember which contest it was." Christy flopped back onto the hay with her arms crossed under her head. "But someday I'm going to get to all those places."

Matt stretched out next to her with his head propped on one hand. His eyes were tender as he gazed down at her delicate face. "I'd like to share the wonder when your dream is realized." He stroked her cheek gently. "If things were different I'd take you there myself."

She stared up into his darkened eyes, feeling a strange flutter in the pit of her stomach. "That would be nice," she whispered.

"It would be heaven! I want to see the world through your eyes. I'd like to climb the Eiffel Tower with you, and take a gondola ride on the Grand Canal. I wish I could buy you something in every shop on the Via Veneto."

Christy touched his high cheekbone tentatively. "You wouldn't need to do that. I'd just like to have you with me."

"Ah, Christy," he groaned. "Sweet, adorable, innocent Christy."

His mouth closed over hers with a restrained kind of hunger, but when she put her arms around his neck, the bonds snapped. Matt pulled her slender body against him and wrapped one leg around both of hers so she was joined to the full, hard length of him.

He parted her lips for a deep kiss that sent shock waves through Christy. She arched her body instinctively, tightening her arms around his neck. Without relinquishing possession of her mouth, Matt unzipped Christy's parka and pulled her inside his jacket.

The heat of his body turned smoldering embers to a torrid blaze. She twined shaking fingers through his thick dark hair as a primitive need engulfed her. Matt's rigid thighs responded automatically, pinning her even closer. Every taut muscle made its impression on her yielding legs. She was completely, willingly enveloped by him. Even their heartbeats merged in a wild thunder.

"You're unbelievable," he murmured, caressing her lingeringly. "My darling, passionate Christy."

She pulled his head down again, lifting her face for another drugging kiss. The glimpse of paradise he'd shown her made Christy eager to enter. Her lips parted in anticipation as his hands moved sensuously over her body.

Matt's kiss was even more urgent this time. He rolled her onto her back without letting her out of his arms. His tense body half covered hers. As his mouth continued its inflaming seduction, he slowly unfastened the top buttons of her shirt. Christy quivered when his hand slipped inside to stroke her intimately. She flamed in his arms, uttering tiny sounds of pleasure.

"I've never wanted anyone so much in my life," he muttered against her mouth.

"I want you too, Matt." Her palms moved over his chest, tracing the broad triangle down to his narrow waist.

He groaned. "You don't know what you're saying."

"Yes, I do," she whispered.

"Are you *sure*, Christy?" He anchored his hands in her bright hair, staring down at her intently.

"Can't you tell?" She looked up at him with wide, trusting eyes. "I've never felt like this before."

The excitement died from his expression. He lowered his head and closed his eyes. "Oh, God, what am I doing!"

"Matt?" She touched his hair tentatively. "What's wrong?"

He looked at her then, but all the passion was gone. "You're a virgin, aren't you, Christy?"

Her cheeks turned a bright, rosy pink. "I . . . does it matter?"

He stood up abruptly and turned his back to her, running a shaking hand through his hair. "Yes, it matters a great deal! I'm not usually in the habit of seducing virgins." His voice was almost savage.

"But you didn't," she faltered. "I wanted ... I mean ..."

"Forget everything I ever told you," he said bitingly. "Stay in Pine Grove for the rest of your life where you'll be safe from men like me."

Christy's long lashes swept down to veil her misery and embarrassment. She had offered herself and been turned down. The reason was just as insulting! Matt was appalled by her lack of experience. He didn't want to be bothered with such a naive innocent. When she'd responded so willingly, he'd gotten the wrong impression. But that wasn't her fault. He could make an angel turn in her wings!

"Thanks for the advice," Christy said bitterly, buttoning her shirt with trembling fingers. "Also, the hands-on demonstration. It was quite an object lesson."

He stared down morosely as she pulled on her boots. "Don't you see what—"

"You can go back to the house now," she interrupted. "I'll finish the chores alone."

"No, *I'll* do them. I feel the need for some exercise," he said grimly.

Christy didn't argue. All she wanted was to put distance between them. Her eyes were shadowed as she entered the kitchen a few minutes later. Fortunately, Sarah was busy at the stove and didn't notice.

"Done so soon? Where's Matt?" she asked.

"He's finishing up. I came back to help you."

"The turkey's already in the oven, and the vegetables are all cleaned." Sarah glanced at the clock.

"You'd better change clothes. We'll open the presents when Matt gets back."

"Why don't we do that after he leaves?"

"I asked him to stay over tonight."

"You didn't!"

Sarah misunderstood her niece's concern. "It's all right. There's a present for him under the tree. I always have a few extra lying around, just in case."

"Don't you think you're carrying this hospitality thing too far?" Christy asked tautly.

"It's Christmas," the older woman chided. "You're supposed to love your fellow man."

"With some notable exceptions," Christy muttered, stalking out of the room.

Sarah stared after her thoughtfully. She was putting out potato chips and dip when Matt came into the kitchen a little later.

"What did you and Christy argue about?" she asked without preamble.

Matt stiffened in the act of taking off his jacket. "What makes you thing we argued?"

"She came in here madder than a bee that got locked out of the hive."

He recovered his poise. "I'm afraid that's my fault. I have a bad habit of giving unwanted advice."

Sarah raised her eyebrows in disbelief. "I may be old, but I'm not completely out of it. Did you make a pass at my niece?"

"It was inexcusable," Matt admitted with a sigh. "Do you want me to leave?"

"Not necessarily. Did anything come of it?"

"No." He looked her squarely in the eye.

"That's all right, then."

"I don't understand you!" Matt jammed his hands in his pockets, tightening the jeans over his strong thighs. "A complete stranger says he made a pass at your niece, and you say it's all right!"

"I didn't say I was delighted," she remarked dryly.

"If you had any sense, you'd throw me out on my ear!" he stormed.

"That wouldn't be easy." She smiled, looking at the long length of him. Her face became serious as she said, "You aren't the first man to be attracted to her, and you won't be the last. Christy's a big girl, Matt. She has to learn to take care of herself. I won't be around to do it forever."

"You haven't done a very good job so far," he said grimly. "She's too trusting. Didn't you ever teach her the facts of life?"

"So that's the way it was," Sarah said softly.

His eyes became hooded. "I don't know what you're talking about."

"You're a good boy, Matt. I'm glad my faith in you wasn't misplaced."

He swore under his breath, stalking out of the room the way Christy had.

Christy changed to a cherry-colored wool dress, wondering how she was going to face Matt after that disgraceful incident in the barn. If only he'd have the decency to leave. She knew her aunt wouldn't hear of it though, unless she told her the truth. And Christy couldn't bring herself to do that. Let the older woman have her illusions. Why should both of theirs be shattered?

The afternoon Christy dreaded wasn't as bad as she had anticipated. Sarah's presence made the gift ex-

changing ceremony bearable, and after people began
dropping by, it was easy to avoid Matt. The only difficulty came when some of Christy's friends wanted to
meet him.

"He's gorgeous, Chris," her friend Irma gushed.
"Who is he?"

Christy shrugged. "One of Aunt Sarah's stray dogs."

"I'll adopt him any day." Irma rolled her eyes ex-
pressively.

"How do you know he doesn't bite?" Christy asked
distantly.

Irma grinned. "I hope he does."

After a brief introduction, Christy left them alone.
She was annoyed to find her eyes returning often to the
alcove where Irma had maneuvered Matt. Christy told
herself that her inattention to old Mrs. Margolin's account of her arthritic knee was only because it was so
boring. But there was no explanation for the pain she
felt as she watched Matt smile down at her friend in-
dulgently.

Christy was in the kitchen replenishing the punch
bowl when he joined her unexpectedly. It was the first
time they'd been alone all afternoon. She started to pick
up the bowl and leave, but Matt took it from her.

"I want to apologize, Christy." His voice was very
gentle.

"For what?" she asked tautly. "Not making love to
me?"

When she tried to brush by him, Matt put his hands
on her shoulders. "No, that's the one thing I've done
right since I got here. You would have regretted it bitterly."

Would she? As Christy stared up at the strong planes
of his hawklike face, she wasn't sure. Even now, after

her humiliation, his touch was making her legs weak. Wouldn't it be worth anything to experience the ecstasy this man could bring?

As though he read her mind, Matt said, "You're too fine a person to indulge in . . . a brief encounter."

"I never—" Her eyelashes fluttered down. He already knew that!

"That's the reason I couldn't take advantage of you. I created a need in you because I was selfish and thoughtless." He brushed the soft hair off her forehead with caressing fingers. "You didn't really want me, honey."

"You needn't try to make me feel better," Christy said miserably. "We both know you were the one who lost interest."

He looked at her incredulously. "You can't honestly believe that?" He clasped her in his arms and rested his cheek on her temple. "Dear heart, it's taking all of my willpower not to carry you off to bed this minute!"

Did he really mean it? Christy looked up at him in confusion. She was so sure it was her inexperience that had turned him off.

Matt stared at her for a long moment, as though memorizing her lovely features. Then he released her. "Forget about me, honey. I'm not real. And neither are you," he muttered under his breath. "This is just a Christmas dream."

Sarah came in while they were gazing at each other wordlessly. She made a small sound of annoyance. "I sent you for that punch ages ago, Christy!"

"I'll carry it in," Matt said, lifting the heavy bowl.

"Come along, Christy," Sarah called over her shoulder. "We have guests."

Christy followed slowly, her thoughts in a turmoil. Matt's explanation of why he'd rejected her made Christy feel better, but telling her to forget him didn't. No matter what he said, she would never forget this charismatic man, even though he'd touched her life only briefly.

After the guests left, they had dinner in the dining room. It was very festive, with candles and a center-piece of poinsettias on the table. Matt was effortlessly charming, prompting Sarah to tell stories about her various activities. He also drew Christy out by asking questions about her job in Squaw Valley, and her friends in Pine Grove. He even seemed interested.

"If you're trying to find out if she has a steady boy-friend, why don't you come right out and ask her?" Sarah said bluntly.

"Can't you see he's just trying to be polite?" Christy scolded.

Matt smiled at the older woman. "I'm sure that's the first thing you would have told me."

She smiled back. "Well, maybe the second. Christy is very popular, though. She's just choosy."

Matt's enigmatic gaze rested on Christy's perturbed face. "Anyone that beautiful deserves to be."

"Will you two stop talking about me as though I weren't here?" she asked crossly. "I'd like to change the subject."

To her great relief, they complied. When the conversation became general once more, Christy relaxed and began to enjoy herself again. It was only much later that she realized Matt hadn't revealed anything about himself. Other than the fact that he was an engineer, they didn't know any more about him than they had when he rang the doorbell. Maybe he really *was* a dream, a Christmas gift that was only on loan.

The evening passed quickly, with much laughter and a warm feeling of companionship. The tension between herself and Matt had vanished. Christy had never spent a happier holiday. The only thing marring it was the knowledge that the next morning Matt would be gone, and she'd almost certainly never see him again.

Christy discovered that time was even more fleeting than she thought.

When it was time for bed, Matt said to Sarah, "How can I begin to thank you for your hospitality?"

"There's no need. We were happy to have you."

"I don't know what I would have done if you hadn't taken me in," he said simply.

"You would have survived." She looked appraisingly at the strong line of his jaw. "I have a feeling you always manage to land on your feet."

He smiled. "Not without a little help from my friends."

"We all need that. It's what Christmas is all about."

Matt's smile was replaced by deep emotion. "You're a remarkable woman, Sarah Blake. It's been a privilege to know you."

"No need to make a speech," Sarah said tartly, although it was clear that she was pleased. "You'll just have to do it all over again after breakfast."

He shook his head. "I'm leaving early."

Christy's face mirrored her dismay. She masked it quickly when Matt turned and took both her hands in a warm grip.

"Goodbye, Christy. It's been a privilege to know you, too." His voice was husky. "I hope you get all the good things you deserve out of life."

* * *

The auto club couldn't give Matt a definite time when
they would show up to tow his car. They only promised
it would be some time in the morning. Matt was there
almost as soon as it was light, in order not to miss them.

The Jaguar had a generous icing of snow after a day
and a half. Was that all it had been? He could hardly
believe it. Surely he'd known Christy longer than that!
She was more familiar to him than girls he'd taken out
for months. The perfume of her skin lingered in his
nostrils, and he could almost feel the silky texture of her
glorious, pale blond hair.

Matt shook his head in disgust. That kind of thinking was for schoolboys, and he was far removed from
that category. He took a tree branch and scraped away
the snow so he could wait inside the car.

It was reasonably warm inside, but there was nothing to do. He had books in his luggage, but that meant
scraping away more snow to get the trunk open. It
didn't seem worth the effort since the tow truck might
come at any moment. Only it didn't. As the time ticked
away, Matt was alone with his thoughts, which kept returning to Christy.

She was a revelation to him. Matt hadn't known girls
like her still existed. She was so sweet and pliant. He
shifted restlessly as memories surfaced. The way she'd
responded to him, the satin feel of her breasts, her shy
delight as he awakened her.

Matt swore softly. It wasn't like him to lose control,
especially when he knew how innocent she was. It would
have been unforgivable if he'd taken her. At least that
was something to be grateful for. It was bad enough that
he'd lied to her and Sarah. Well, not lied actually. It was

more a sin of omission. He'd *wanted* to tell them the truth about himself, but something always prevented it.

Matt sighed. Well, it was all over. He'd never see either of them again. It would be madness to stay in touch. He had used up all of his nobility when he'd resisted Christy the first time. Matt didn't trust himself to pass up another opportunity—and she deserved better.

His secretary was surprised when Matt showed up at the office early the next day. "I thought you went skiing." She followed him into the plush inner office that was furnished almost like an elegant den.

"I came back," he said curtly. He frowned at a pile of unopened envelopes on the big mahogany desk. "Have I been promoted to mail clerk around here?"

Her eyes widened at his bad temper. Matt was usually the soul of courtesy. "Those are personal. I thought you'd prefer to open your own Christmas cards."

He pushed the envelopes aside indifferently. "Get your book, Linda. I'd like you to do a couple of things for me."

When she was seated in front of his desk, Matt said, "I want to send a ten pound box of chocolates to Sarah and Christy Blake in Pine Grove. It's near Squaw Valley. I don't know the address, but it's just a little town. I guess it will get to them."

"No problem, I'll locate the address. What do you want me to say on the card?"

"I'll write it myself." He looked at her broodingly. "On second thought, make that a five pound box instead." It wouldn't do to look too affluent.

She made a notation. "Anything else?"

"Yes. Have some stationery printed with the name and address of one of the big cereal companies—Kellogg's or Post, any of the big ones will do."

"A cereal company?" Linda's brows climbed incredulously.

"Just do it!" Matt said impatiently.

It was so unlike him that she was worried. He looked kind of drawn, too. "Do you feel all right?"

As his eyes met her concerned ones, Matt sighed. "I'm sorry, Linda. I didn't mean to be so abrupt. I guess I am rather out of sorts. My car got wrecked and I had to wait two hours for a tow truck. I never did get to Squaw Valley."

"What a shame! You were all alone on Christmas?"

"No, some wonderful people took me in," he said softly.

"It wasn't like being with your friends, though."

His mouth twisted in the semblance of a smile. "No, it wasn't anything like that."

"Well, you can make up for it New Year's Eve," she consoled him. "Miss Warren phoned and left a message that you're invited to two cocktail parties before the dinner dance at the country club."

Mimi Warren was a beautiful blonde. That was the only thing she and Christy had in common. Matt contemplated the coming festivities without enthusiasm. He hadn't escaped the Christmas parties, merely postponed them. It would be the same boring rounds. Even the conclusion of the evening was predictable. The only question was whether they would wind up in Mimi's bed or his own.

"How much stationery do you want printed?" Linda got back to business.

"Whatever's necessary. I only need one sheet." He turned his back on her surprised face. "Use it to write a letter to Miss Christy Blake in Pine Grove. The letter will read: 'Dear Miss Blake, we are pleased to inform you that you have won first prize in our grand sweepstakes contest, a two week, all expense paid cruise to the Caribbean aboard the *Sun Queen*.' " He paused to collect his thoughts. " 'Please contact the local steamship office in San Francisco to arrange for the trip at your convenience.' Sign that, um, Jonathan Ridgely, President, Contest Division."

Linda managed a businesslike expression, although she was bursting with curiosity. "Will that be all?"

"I want it sent immediately."

"It's going to take a little time. Today's Friday."

"So?"

"The weekend's coming, and then New Year's. Not much gets done between the holidays."

"Pay extra for a rush job," he said impatiently. "I want that letter to go out as soon as possible. And arrange for a deluxe cabin in Miss Blake's name. Pay for it out of my personal account."

After Linda had gone, Matt walked to the window to stare out at the gray day that matched his mood. His debt was discharged. Would the trip make Christy as happy as she expected? He hoped so.

"God, I'd like to take it with her!" he muttered.

Chapter Three

Matt tried to control his temper that Friday, but everything irritated him. The people in the office walked softly, raising their eyebrows at one another in perplexity.

Friday night wasn't any more rewarding. In an effort to banish Christy from his thoughts, Matt called Mimi Warren.

"Darling, how wonderful!" she exclaimed. "I didn't expect you back so soon. You must have missed me."

"It wasn't the same without you," he answered dryly.

"You're a dear! I can't *wait* to see you. You're coming to the Debenham's tonight, aren't you? I was going with Tommy Armistead, but I'll make up some excuse."

"How would you like to go out for a quiet dinner instead?"

"Oh, lover, I'd adore it, but I couldn't possibly. Pat Stillman has already described my gown in tomorrow's column."

"I didn't realize," Matt said with exaggerated remorse. "We can't let the society editor down, can we?"

"Don't be cross, darling." Mimi's voice dropped to a suggestive purr. "The party won't last all night."

She couldn't believe it when Matt refused to accompany her. After coaxing was useless, she stifled her annoyance and said regretfully, "If there was any way I could get out of this thing you know I would, sweetie, but I'll make it up to you New Year's Eve.''

Matt hung up feeling curiously relieved. He wondered what Christy was doing.

Christy wasn't in any better a mood.

"You've been moping around the house all day, child!" Sarah exclaimed in exasperation. "Why didn't you go to the movies with Craig Selby when he asked you?"

"I didn't feel like it." Christy's soft mouth drooped. "I have a headache."

Sarah suspected it was more like a heartache, but she didn't say so. "Well, take some aspirin and go to bed."

"It's only seven-thirty!"

"Then read a book, or watch television." Sarah went back to her crossword puzzle.

Christy picked up a magazine and sat down across from her aunt. She flipped through the pages disconsolately. "It's so depressing after Christmas." She sighed.

"There's always New Year's Eve to look forward to."

"I suppose so."

"I want you youngsters to be careful driving back from Squaw Valley. There are all kinds of nuts out on New Year's Eve." Sarah hadn't been happy about Christy's plans to go to a dance at the lodge with a group of friends, but she made it a practice not to interfere.

"Craig is a safe driver." Christy stared moodily into the crackling fire. "He does everything safely. I don't think he's ever taken a chance in his life."

"You're hardly one to talk," Sarah said quietly.

Christy threw down the magazine and stood up. "Sometimes I think you want to get rid of me!"

"You know better than that," Sarah said calmly. "I only want what's best for you. Just because my life is here in Pine Grove doesn't mean you have to waste yours. There's a whole world out there, child!"

"You sound like Matt," Christy muttered.

"He's a very astute young man."

"You don't know anything about him!" Christy exclaimed in outrage. "He could be a criminal on the run for all we know. Did you notice the way he avoided talking about himself?"

"He probably had his reasons."

"You're too trusting," Christy scolded.

"Strange." Sarah penciled in a word. "He said the same thing about you."

Christy's cheeks flamed as she recalled her total surrender in Matt's arms. "Doesn't that give you some idea of the kind of women he's accustomed to?" she asked coldly.

"Satisfied ones, I imagine."

"Aunt Sarah!"

"There's no point in denying that he's a charming devil." The older woman looked thoughtful. "It will be interesting to see what he makes of himself."

"We'll never know," Christy said forlornly.

"I'm not so sure. I have a feeling we'll hear from Matt Destry again."

Matt was up early Saturday morning after a very dull evening of watching television. He felt keyed up and restless, so he called a friend and made a date for handball. That, at least, was satisfying. After a strenuous workout, he felt better, but the rest of the day and night stretched ahead like a vacuum.

About two in the afternoon, he faced his problem squarely. Christy had become an obsession. He was romanticizing one brief encounter. The unexpected circumstances, the storybook setting, everything had conspired to make their meeting something it wasn't. She was breathtakingly lovely, but he had known literally dozens of beautiful women. He and Christy had absolutely nothing in common. If he saw her again, he'd be disappointed.

Matt's eyes brightened as the idea took hold. That was what he needed—an exorcism! And while he was at it, he'd set the record straight about himself. The inadvertent deception continued to bother him.

Matt looked at his watch. He could be in Pine Grove before dinner. The Jaguar was in the repair shop, but that was only a minor hitch. He'd borrow one of the vans from CompuTrend's motor pool.

Christy was staring listlessly out at the snow. That was another depressing thing about winter. It was already dark, even though it was only five-thirty.

A strange van pulled into the driveway. She looked at it curiously, trying to make out the lettering on the side, but the light was too dim. A delivery at this hour? A man got out and walked toward the front door.

For a moment Christy thought he was a figment of her own wishful imagination, but there was no mistaking that broad-shouldered male frame, or the easy gliding walk. It was Matt!

She opened the door and raced out into the snow, throwing her arms around his neck. "You came back!"

His arms closed around her automatically, holding her so tightly that she could hear his heart pound. She clung to him, inhaling his familiar clean scent.

"I couldn't stay away." His mouth slid sensuously over her cheek. "Did you miss me?"

Christy drew back self-consciously. She was suddenly aware of her impulsive actions. "I . . . we wondered how you were doing."

"Not too great." The starlight was reflected in his navy eyes, making them glitter as he gazed at her lovely face.

It was all happening again, the mounting excitement, the inexpressible feeling that made her tremble.

"You're shivering. Come inside before you catch cold." Cradling her body against his for warmth, Matt led her to the house.

Christy moved to the fireplace while he took off his storm coat. She was startled to see that he was wearing a shirt and tie under a camel-hair jacket. The well-tailored slacks that completed the outfit were a far cry from his former blue jeans. He looked elegant and sophisticated, not at all like a man down on his luck.

"You look different," she said tentatively.

"You don't." He came to stand over her. "You're just as I remembered."

"It's only been two days."

"It has to be longer," he murmured huskily.

Christy tried valiantly to stem the rising tide of desire. She mustn't make a fool of herself again. "I'm sorry that things aren't going well for you, but it doesn't show. You're extremely dashing," she said lightly.

"I didn't say things weren't going well." He frowned slightly. "That's part of the reason I came back."

"You got a job!" Christy's face lit up. "Oh, Matt, I'm so happy for you."

"It isn't what you think," he began.

"I don't care what kind of job it is. You'll work your way up."

Matt couldn't go through with it when he looked at her glowing face. "Will you have dinner with me tonight? Aunt Sarah, too."

Maybe an opening would come up during the evening, he thought distractedly. Nothing was going according to plan. The minute Christy launched herself into his arms, he knew it had been a mistake to come. The remembered feeling of her curved body mocked all his theories. She could never be a disappointment.

"Aunt Sarah's at a Ladies Aid meeting, but I'd love to go," Christy said. "Give me ten minutes to change clothes."

Christy left her sweater and jeans in an untidy pile, which she never usually did. After a brief deliberation, she chose the most sophisticated thing in her closet, a black knit dress with tiny pearls scattered over the bodice. It clung to her faultless figure like a second skin, and the matching high-heeled sling pumps flattered her long, slim legs. A few more moments were spent freshening her makeup and brushing her hair to a shining halo.

Something smoldered in Matt's eyes as he viewed the result. "That was fast."

Christy's laughter bubbled up spontaneously. "I didn't want you to change your mind."

"Is that your opinion of me, that I'm an Indian giver?" he teased.

"No, you've always been honorable with me." She meant it as a joke, but the memorable incident in the barn leaped to both their minds.

Matt's smile vanished. "In all the ways that count, anyway."

She bit her lip nervously. "Do you . . . Where would you like to eat? There isn't a wide choice in Pine Grove."

His urbanity returned. "I thought we'd drive to Squaw Valley. If you don't mind riding in a van, that is."

"It's fine with me, but we can take my car if you'd rather. I had the heater fixed."

"Maybe you'd be more comfortable. Do you mind if I drive?"

She handed him the keys, smiling. "Did my driving the other night scare you?"

"No, I was impressed with the way you handled the pickup on those icy roads. I'm just one of those insecure males who has to be in charge of a date."

"You don't strike me as being insecure," she commented as he opened the car door.

"It's a recent development," he answered dryly.

When they reached Squaw Valley, Matt pulled into the parking lot of the chalet. It had a coffee shop and a more formal dining room where there was dancing. He guided Christy toward the dining room.

She held back. "It's too expensive in there. Let's go to the coffee shop."

"This is a special occasion," Matt said easily. "I want to toast you with champagne."

"You can do that with apple cider. It's the same color, and a lot cheaper."

"Indulge me. I feel like celebrating."

"You don't know how expensive it is," she protested. "I had lunch here once and it was outrageous. I can just imagine what the dinner prices are like!"

He put his hands on her shoulders, gazing deeply into her eyes. "I want to do so much for you, Christy, and I can't. Let me have this evening."

It was at that moment that Christy realized she was in love with Matt. She had thought it was just a physical attraction, but it was so much more. He was everything she'd ever wanted in a man—tender, thoughtful, generous. It touched her that he wanted to give her things. If only he knew there was just one thing she wanted—him. Was it possible? He *had* come back, after a very final sounding goodbye. Christy was filled with hope as she followed Matt silently.

The maître d' led them to a choice table by the window where they could look out at the flaming torches that added a touch of color to the black-and-white landscape.

"Would you care for cocktails, sir?" The man's manner was respectful.

When Christy shook her head, Matt said, "I think we'll have wine instead. Will you send over the wine steward? Oh, and a guest menu too, if you have one."

"Certainly, sir."

Christy looked puzzled. "What's a guest menu?"

Matt smiled. "Something special for beautiful ladies."

He wouldn't tell her any more, but she discovered the difference for herself. "There aren't any prices!" she exclaimed.

"I want you to enjoy your dinner." He grinned.

"How can I when every bite is probably the equivalent of a dollar bill?"

"The dollar isn't worth what it used to be anyway. Just tell yourself you're providing a lot of people with jobs."

"It's a good thing *you* have one, although at the rate you're spending your advance, you're going to be poor for a long time yet."

A curtain dropped behind his dark eyes. "What if I told you I was rich?"

"I'd tell you money doesn't matter to me," she said gently. "I like you just the way you are."

"But what if it was really true?" he asked intently.

A slight frown marred Christy's smooth forehead as she considered the question. "I suppose I'd be very angry."

"Why?"

"Because it would mean you were making fun of us," she said slowly. "That you were secretly laughing at our small town ways."

"You couldn't possibly believe that!"

She looked at him uncertainly. "It would hurt a lot, but I don't really know anything about you. *Are* you rich, Matt?"

A muscle twitched at the point of his square jaw as he said, "I've never lied to you, Christy."

It was true, even if it was an evasion. How could he admit everything now? The web of deception was like a noose around his neck.

"You came from a wealthy family though, didn't you?" she asked. It would explain his assurance in what should have been foreign surroundings.

"They were comfortable," Matt admitted.

Christy hesitated. "You've never mentioned your family or friends. Is there a reason, Matt?"

His firm mouth twisted in a rueful smile. "I don't have a lurid past, if that's what you mean."

"But you don't want to talk about yourself." It was a cross between a question and a statement.

"Not tonight. I have a few problems to work out first." He reached over and took her hands. "This night is special. I don't want anything to ruin it."

Christy couldn't help wondering if Matt was hiding some dark secret, in spite of his reassurances. But when she looked into his steady eyes, it didn't seem possible. Even though she knew very little about him, Christy was sure he couldn't do anything dishonorable.

"Are you ready to order, sir?" The appearance of the waiter broke the tense atmosphere.

Matt knew that Christy was trying to figure out the least expensive thing on the menu, so he ordered for both of them. "We'll have oysters on the half shell, endive salad and steak Diane."

"Very good, sir," the man said. "And would you like a soufflé for dessert? It has to be ordered ahead of time."

"Excellent idea. We'll have a Grand Marnier soufflé. And you can pour the champagne now."

Christy watched wonderingly as Matt discussed vintages with the wine steward. His ease in the plush surroundings and the deference accorded to him were a revelation. Matt must have lived very well at one time.

"Tell me about your new job," she prompted when the waiter left. "Was that a company car you were driving? I saw some writing on the side, but I couldn't make out the name."

"CompuTrend," he answered briefly. "It's an electronics firm."

"That was exactly what you wanted! What do you do there?"

"A little bit of everything—like you." He shifted the focus of the conversation deftly. "Now that I think of it, this is something of a busman's holiday for you. You commute to Squaw Valley every day. Perhaps we should have had dinner in Pine Grove."

"You wouldn't have gotten anything like this."

Matt smiled. "It's the company, not the cuisine."

Christy laughed self-consciously. "I'd have to be very charming to make up for the food at the Elite Café."

"All you ever have to be is yourself." His voice dropped a note. "Don't ever change, Christy."

"Everyone changes," she said slowly. "It's part of maturing."

His gaze wandered over her delicate features. "You're perfect just as you are."

Christy dimly realized that for some reason, Matt had put her on a pedestal. "I'm a real person, Matt," she said urgently. "Not a princess in an ivory tower. I'm no different from the women you know."

Mimi Warren flashed into his mind, the games she played, her shallow values. "You couldn't be more wrong," he said.

"Tell me how I'm different—besides the fact that they have more experience." Christy's cheeks flushed, but her eyes held his.

Matt answered her question with one of his own. "What do you like to do in your free time?"

"Oh . . . ski in the winter, swim and play tennis in the summer."

"And in the evening?" he prompted.

"The same as anyone else I suppose—go to parties and movies with my friends. Not every night, though. Sometimes I just like to stay home and read."

"Have you ever gone to three parties in one night?"

She looked at him in surprise. "Why would anyone want to do that?"

The music started and Matt drew her to her feet. "I've just won my case," he said with satisfaction.

Christy accompanied him to the dance floor with a dozen unanswered questions churning around in her mind. Had she passed the test or flunked it? Did Matt enjoy an endless round of activities? Christy couldn't help knowing that he was attracted to her physically, but other than that, did he consider her boring?

When she slipped into his arms, the questions faded in importance. She relaxed against him, letting her senses take over. Matt didn't talk either. His hands trailed over her back, tracing its slender lines. They communicated wordlessly, moving as one person. Her body responded to every direction of his.

There was an awesome kind of chemistry between them that couldn't be denied. When Matt drew her closer and kissed her closed eyelids, Christy knew he was making love to her in the only way he would permit himself.

She sighed unconsciously, and he tilted her chin up. "What's wrong, sweetheart?"

She opened her eyes and gazed into his beloved face. "Nothing. I was just wishing..."

"What?" he asked when she stopped. "Tell me what it is, and I'll get it for you," he said urgently.

It wasn't that easy; you couldn't ask someone to fall in love with you. "Christmas is over." She managed a smile.

Matt smoothed a shining strand of hair behind her ear in a caressing gesture. "Maybe I can catch Santa Claus before he goes back to the North Pole."

"He gave me enough already," Christy said softly.

The music ended and they went back to their table.

It was a bittersweet evening. Every moment was precious because Christy didn't know if this was all there would be. Matt hadn't mentioned any future meetings. Would he disappear again and not return? She shook off the depression that caused. It was all the more reason to enjoy what time she had with him.

Christy had left a message for her aunt, telling where she'd gone. When they returned home, Sarah was in bed, but there was a note saying she'd made up the guest room for Matt.

"That was thoughtful of her, but I didn't expect to stay," he said.

"It's a three-hour drive," Christy protested. "You wouldn't get home until two-thirty."

"I've been up that late before." He smiled. "But I would like to see Aunt Sarah again. That's one wise lady."

"Who would be furious if I let you take that long drive at this hour. So it's all settled."

Matt grinned. "You talked me into it. Pretty soon I'll have to start paying rent."

"Or keep a spare pair of pajamas here."

"I don't use them."

An all too vivid picture of his naked male body sprang to Christy's mind. She had felt its hard contours often enough to provide all the details. Her cheeks warmed at the memory. "Well, uh, that's fortunate."

"I can't believe you're blushing! A lot of people sleep in the nude, honey."

"I know," she mumbled. Christy couldn't tell him that wasn't the reason for her high color.

"I should have expected it from a little puritan who wears a high-necked flannel gown to bed," he teased.

"I get cold," she muttered.

Matt's laughter died, and tiny pinpoints of light appeared in his navy eyes. "That's a pity," he said softly.

"It's my own fault. I should get an electric blanket," she murmured.

He didn't appear to hear her. Hooking a hand around her neck, he drew her closer. "I'd like to keep you warm, sweetheart. I'd like to hold your beautiful body in my arms all night. I want to kiss every inch of your satin skin and be the one to make you come alive."

Christy stared into his hypnotic eyes, feeling a throbbing in her midsection. Matt had made love to her in every way but the ultimate one. Was this the magic moment? Did she want it to be, knowing he'd be regretful afterward, even if she wouldn't?

He pulled her into his arms and kissed her almost savagely. "You're like a fever in my blood," he groaned. "I've never felt like this about a woman."

The minute his lips touched hers, all other considerations became unimportant. Christy feathered tiny kisses over the strong column of his throat. "Why does it bother you, darling? We want each other. Isn't that enough?" She loosened his tie and unfastened the top buttons of his shirt.

"Oh, God, don't do that!" he exclaimed as her fingers slipped inside to tangle in the thick mat of hair on his chest.

"I've wanted to for such a long time." She sighed, feeling sensual pleasure at the evidence of his masculinity.

"It's all wrong," he groaned, but his hand cupped her breast and his thumb circled the hardened tip.

Christy quivered as an inexpressive feeling kindled her body. "Tell me why," she whispered.

"I don't want to hurt you, don't you understand?"

"I know you'll be gentle," she murmured.

"That's not what I meant. Of course I'd be gentle! But I can't take what you have to give."

She rubbed her cheek against the crisp hair on his chest while she unbuttoned his shirt further. "I'm not asking for anything in return."

"You should be!" He wrenched her chin up and stared at her with blazing eyes. "Don't throw yourself away on someone like me. I'm not worth it!"

"Love me, Matt." Her angelic face was entreating. "Just for tonight."

"How can I resist?" he muttered hoarsely.

He swung her into his arms and captured her mouth for a deep, rousing kiss. Christy's fingers twined through his thick hair as she strained against him. She was on fire with love for this man, who was everything she had always dreamed of. It didn't matter at this moment that he didn't love her in return. She had to experience fulfillment in his arms, no matter what heartbreak came after.

Matt carried her slowly down the hall, as though prolonging the exquisite moment. His hands and mouth fed the excitement. While his lips wandered over her face and neck, his fingertips tantalized her body, arousing her with their intimate exploration. Christy moaned softly, digging her nails into the taut muscles of his back.

As they approached her room, a loud snore ripped through the stillness. It was a note of reality in an unreal world. They had both forgotten Christy's aunt. Their eyes met in consternation.

Matt lowered her to her feet. "This isn't the place," he murmured.

"No." Christy couldn't look at him.

She turned away, but he pulled her into his arms and kissed her briefly. "I'm sorry, sweetheart."

Christy undressed quickly and huddled under the covers, feeling waves of shame wash over her. Matt was certainly right—this *wasn't* the place! What if Aunt Sarah had awakened and come to ask if... Christy turned over and buried her face in the pillow.

It was unthinkable! She would be so disappointed. The older woman was very open-minded in most ways, but her generation was extremely rigid in its thinking about certain things. She wouldn't understand that Christy had fallen hopelessly in love with Matt, that she wanted to belong to him in every way.

Was he lying in bed across the hall in the darkness, aching with the same longing? Or was he relieved? Matt's conscience was formidable. It had failed him for a short time tonight, but that wasn't really his fault. He had tried to hold back, even though his need was as great as hers. Why? Why did he treat her so differently from other women?

Matt was sitting up in bed with his arms folded, asking himself the same question. What was there about Christy that tied him up in knots? She was driving him over the edge with wanting her, yet he couldn't take her. Why?

"She's so innocent!" Matt groaned aloud.

But at least he'd initiate her gently. Another man might not. The thought made him rake rigid fingers through his hair. Matt considered himself an honorable man. He had never seduced a woman. They had all been consenting adults. Christy certainly met the requirements. Why did he feel this urge to protect her at all costs? That was an emotion reserved for the woman you loved.

Matt got out of bed to pace the floor restlessly. The idea was too idiotic to consider! You didn't fall in love with someone you'd known exactly one day and two nights. The only thing involved here was basic sex. He had been attracted to Christy instantly, and the itch had grown stronger. It was sex that had brought him back to Pine Grove, but common sense would see to it that he never returned!

Only one person in the house got any sleep that night.

Chapter Four

Matt was in the kitchen with Sarah when Christy joined them the next morning. He was sprawled in a wooden chair with his long legs stretched out, laughing at something the older woman had said. Christy's breath caught in her throat at how handsome he was. His shirt was open at the collar, and his cuffs were rolled halfway up his well-developed forearms. He presented a strikingly virile picture.

"There you are, sleepyhead." Sarah turned and saw Christy in the doorway. "Did Matt keep you out too late last night?"

"No, he, uh, we got home before midnight." Christy's swift glance at him wasn't encouraging. Matt's easy laughter had fled, leaving his face almost austere.

"Did you two have a good time?" Sarah asked.

"Why didn't you ask Matt?" Christy went to the cupboard for silver and napkins to set the table.

"I was so busy going on about the argument at the Ladies Aid meeting that I didn't get around to it." She looked appraisingly at him. "You should be one of those interviewers on TV. You have a knack for getting people to talk about themselves."

"He's great on conversation." Christy's tone was biting. "As long as he doesn't have to take part."

Her nerves were wound to the breaking point. Matt's coldness after the night before was insulting. She hadn't thrown herself at him; he'd started it! If he couldn't make up his mind about how he felt, that was *his* problem. At least he could be civil. He hadn't even said good morning to her.

Sarah was looking at her in astonishment. "What's gotten into you this morning? You sound downright cranky."

"I'm afraid it's my fault, and I regret it." Matt's dark eyes were opaque. "I plied her with too much champagne last night, didn't I, Christy?"

He was always trying to give her an out, to pretend that her actions weren't voluntary, but his fault instead. Christy didn't appreciate his gallantry. They both knew the truth of the matter. What Matt didn't know was the reason she responded so readily—that she'd fallen in love with him. That was something he'd *never* know, she vowed.

Sarah glanced from one to the other, shrewdly sizing up the situation. It didn't take a genius to figure out how they felt about each other, but something had gone wrong. They were both suffering mightily. For the first time, Sarah was glad she wasn't young anymore.

Matt left right after breakfast. He politely refused Sarah's invitation to stay, pleading things to do in the city.

"All right, come back and see us soon," Sarah said, ignoring Christy's pointed silence.

"I expect the next few weeks to be rather hectic," he answered evasively.

"I don't doubt it, with the new job and all. Well, don't forget us."

"I'm not likely to." His face was expressionless as he turned to Christy. "Thank you for a delightful evening."

"I enjoyed it, too." She looked back at him with the same lack of emotion.

They were like two strangers, courteously going through the amenities. Sarah's heart went out to both of them.

After he'd gone, she was falsely cheerful. "Well, that was a nice surprise, having Matt drop by like that. Didn't I tell you we'd hear from him?"

Christy kept her head averted as she started to clear the table. "He won't be back."

"Would you like to tell me about it?" her aunt asked quietly, dropping the false gaiety.

"There's nothing to tell."

Sarah sighed. "You're in love with him, aren't you?"

"No!" When the older woman merely gazed at her steadily, Christy picked up some dishes and carried them to the sink. "I'll admit I find him attractive. He's very handsome. But we . . . we don't think alike. I don't want to see him again." She turned on the water, ending the discussion.

Matt concurred heartily: Christy was a closed incident in his life.

That Sunday night he took Diane Cooke to dinner. She was a brunette. On Monday night, after a long day at work, he took a stunning redhead to the opera. Both women were surprised when he dropped each at her respective door afterward.

On Tuesday afternoon, he was the only one in the office.

"It's New Year's Eve," his secretary, Linda, informed him. "What are you still doing here?"

"I have some work to clear up."

"You ought to be home taking a nap." She grinned. "You have a big evening ahead."

"Yes, I suppose so," he said flatly.

"Everyone else has gone," Linda remarked hesitantly. "Do you want me to stick around?"

"No, go ahead. Have a good time tonight."

"You too, boss." Her eyes sparkled with anticipation as she left.

Matt envied her. His face was drawn as he tied his black tie into a precise bow some time later. He felt keyed up, but not with anticipation.

Mimi Warren looked breathtaking when Matt picked her up that evening. Her shining blond hair was swept up on top of her head in an intricate style that had taken the hairdresser hours to arrange. It was worthy of her elegant designer gown, a froth of black lace that showed off her excellent figure to perfection. The low-cut neckline exposed tantalizing glimpses of her full breasts.

"Do you like it?" She twirled for Matt's inspection.

"You're positively ravishing."

Matt looked at the beautiful woman who had shared his bed and felt absolutely nothing. A slender blond girl in jeans and a checkered shirt filled his mind instead.

"Thank you, darling. You look outstanding too." Mimi admired the black and white perfection of his broad-shouldered male form. She put her arms around his neck. "We make a perfect couple," she purred.

"Right." Matt reached for her fur jacket. "Come on, we don't want to be late for the Pomeroys' cocktail party."

It was at the country club, two cocktail parties later, that Matt capitulated. When someone asked Mimi to dance, he went to a pay phone and called Christy.

He let it ring endlessly, but there was no answer. Matt knew his disappointment was out of all proportion. It was New Year's Eve. Of course she wouldn't be sitting at home. He would even have settled for Sarah, though. At least she could have told him where Christy was, and when she'd be home. He called at intervals all evening, but there was never an answer. Matt found it difficult to mask his frustration as the festivities around him grew more frantic.

Christy's evening wasn't any more successful than Matt's.

Her new dress hadn't cost anywhere near what Mimi's had, but it was equally becoming. The peach-colored chiffon gown was both soft and flattering, bringing out golden highlights in her smooth skin. She had washed her hair and combed it into a simple style that floated around her shoulders like a silken curtain.

"You look lovely," Sarah said approvingly.

"Thanks," Christy answered without enthusiasm.

"Do you have your key? I won't be home tonight, remember."

Christy smiled. "I'd never hear the end of it if *I* stayed out all night."

"You wouldn't if you were playing bridge at Rhoda Turner's," Sarah said dryly.

"Just see that you ladies get along," Christy teased. "Those bridge games can get pretty competitive. You don't want to start the new year with a feud."

"Rhoda and I will massacre them," Sarah said calmly.

Christy laughed. "Remember to stop for a minute at twelve o'clock to say happy New Year."

"Don't worry about me. You just have a good time."

Christy's laughter faded. "I will."

"Craig's a nice boy, and he's crazy about you." Sarah hesitated. "It's something to think about. Sometimes it's better to settle for good, honest affection."

"*You* didn't," Christy said soberly.

"And I've been very lonely."

"I'm sorry, Aunt Sarah!"

"That's all right. I wouldn't do anything differently if I had it to do over again. Once you soar with an eagle, you can't settle for a homing pigeon. I think about Fred every day of my life," she said softly.

"Doesn't the memory ever fade?" Christy asked hopelessly.

Sarah regretted her self-indulgent lapse. "Of course it does! I'm just a stubborn old woman who likes living in the past. You're not a bit like me, thank goodness."

The doorbell rang, announcing the arrival of Christy's date. Craig Selby was almost as blond as she, with a perennially boyish face. He seemed a little ill at ease in the unaccustomed formality of a tuxedo, but they made a handsome couple.

"You be careful driving now," Sarah instructed.

"I wouldn't take any chances with this little doll," Craig assured her. He put his arm around Christy's shoulders and drew her against his lanky body.

She couldn't help thinking how different it felt from Matt's powerful male frame. Christy pushed the thought firmly out of her mind. Eagles might soar, but they also destroyed weaker creatures. She didn't intend to become a victim.

All of Christy's friends were at the dance, including some she hadn't seen in a while. There was a lot of animated conversation as everyone exchanged news and gossip. The noise and laughter grew in volume as the hour got later.

At first, Christy enjoyed herself. The party atmosphere was infectious. But as the evening wore on, her pleasure dimmed, especially when Craig began holding her closer.

Christy honestly tried to respond. She like Craig. They had been going out together for a long time, and had a lot of shared interests. Rockets and pinwheels didn't explode when they were together, at least not for her, but it hadn't seemed important—until she met Matt. He taught her what excitement there could be between a man and a woman.

Where was he tonight? Romancing some woman, undoubtedly. Was he telling her how beautiful she was, how exquisite and irresistible? Christy's heart started to pound at the memory of Matt's low, husky voice murmuring those rousing words. But he was whispering them to someone else now.

"Happy New Year, doll." Bells started to peal as Craig put his arms around her. "I'm hoping for big things to happen this year." His mouth covered hers urgently.

Matt would have left the country club after the midnight festivities, but Mimi thought he was joking. He convinced her to leave about two o'clock, after what amounted to a small scene at the dance. It turned uglier when he said good-night at her door without coming in. There had been a lot of recriminations, which Matt only half listened to. His full attention was centered on Christy.

He had called her twice more from the club, and now he was getting tense. Sure, it was New Year's Eve, but not everyone felt they had to stay out all night to prove they'd had a good time. He could hardly wait to get to the telephone again.

When there was no answer at three o'clock, Matt was almost paranoid. Had something happened to her? Had she done something foolish? Matt finally faced what was really bothering him. He knew Christy had felt rejected, in spite of his attempts to explain. Was she spending the night with some man just to prove she was desirable? The thought made a pulse throb at his temple.

When Christy finally answered the phone a little before four, Matt's relief translated into anger. "Where the hell have you been?" he flared.

"Matt?" For a moment she thought she was imagining things, that she had conjured him up out of her longing to hear his voice.

"I asked you a question. *Where were you?*"

"I went to a dance in Squaw Valley." His forcefulness drew the answer out of her.

"Don't you know it's dangerous to be on those mountain roads, tonight of all nights? There are a lot of drunks out there."

"We did see an accident," she admitted. "That's why it took so long to get home."

"What was Sarah thinking about, letting you go to Squaw on a night like this?" he raged.

Reaction was setting in and Christy was becoming annoyed. "Aunt Sarah doesn't tell me what to do, and it's certainly no concern of yours," she said coldly. "Why are you calling at this hour?"

Matt's anger evaporated suddenly. His voice dropped several notes. "I've been thinking of you all evening."

"I'll bet!"

"Did you think about me?" he asked softly.

"Not once," she lied.

"Tell me the truth, sweetheart." His throaty voice was caressing.

"Don't call me that!" she ordered. "I'm not your sweetheart, or anything else. There's nothing between us anymore. There never was," she corrected herself.

"You know that isn't true."

Christy was determined not to let him trap her into remembering. "What do you want, Matt?" she asked bluntly.

"For a long time I didn't know," he said slowly.

"Tell me something I *don't* know!"

"I can't blame you for being angry, honey. I gave you a rough time. But try to understand. I never met anyone like you."

"I guess they sacrificed all the virgins long ago," she answered sardonically. "We're a dying breed."

"That isn't what I meant!"

"Admit it! I scared the daylights out of you," she accused.

"But not for the reason you think. I didn't even understand it myself until tonight."

"Perhaps you'll share this revelation with me."

"I'm in love with you, Christy."

For a moment there was dead silence on the line. Christy couldn't believe he'd said what she'd longed to hear. Incredulous joy filled her—until caution set in. Matt had played games with her before.

"What gives you that idea?" she demanded.

"How do you explain love?" he asked simply. "I can't sleep. My temper's rotten. I can't concentrate. When you put it into words it sounds like flu symptoms."

"Maybe that's what you have," she said hesitantly.

"Darling Christy." He chuckled deeply. "If you were here, I'd show you how healthy I am."

She was filled with confusion. Christy didn't know whether to believe him or not. But why would he lie about something that important? It would be a cruel thing to do if it wasn't true, and that wasn't Matt's nature. Another solution occurred to her.

"How much have you had to drink?" she asked tentatively.

Matt's laughter had a joyous sound. "The only thing I'm drunk on is love. I'm coming up to see you, honey. Wait for me."

"It's almost morning. You'd better get some sleep first," she said anxiously.

"I suppose you're right," he answered reluctantly. "Okay, I'll be there this afternoon."

Christy managed only a few hours sleep herself. She was in the kitchen drinking coffee when Sarah came home late that morning.

"I didn't expect you to be up until noon," Sarah exclaimed. "Was the party a washout?"

"No, it was fun."

Sarah appraised the becoming color in her niece's cheeks, and the sparkle in her blue eyes. "Did you meet anybody new there?"

Christy gave her a brilliant smile. "Just the same old crowd."

Sarah gave it up as a bad job. Something was going on, but Christy would tell her in her own good time. "I intended to tiptoe around, but as long as you're up, I'll make breakfast."

"Not for me," Christy declined. "I have to get dressed."

"Are you going out?" Sarah expressed surprise. Christy usually watched the New Year's Day football games in her robe and slippers.

"No, Matt's coming up."

"How do you know that?"

"He called after I got home last night," Christy said self-consciously.

"I see." Sarah gazed at her for a long moment before making up her mind. Her voice was casual as she said, "I'm glad you'll have company. I just came home to change clothes. I promised Rhoda I'd come back to help her clean up."

Christy wasn't fooled. How much mess could four older ladies make? Did her aunt know what privacy meant to two people in love? Had she had her moment alone with Fred before he went off to war? Christy hoped so.

"Thank you, Aunt Sarah," she said gently.

The older woman stared at her somberly. "I very possibly should have my head examined," she muttered. When Christy's clear blue eyes met hers with confidence, Sarah said dryly, "I was referring to the way Rhoda takes advantage of me."

"I understood that." Christy couldn't suppress a smile.

"I won't be home until dinnertime. Not before five at the very earliest," Sarah warned.

* * *

Christy changed her mind three times before deciding what to wear. Her first impulse was to choose something soft and alluring, but pride wouldn't permit it. Matt could just take her the way she usually dressed at home. That meant jeans and a shirt, but Christy was reluctant to be *that* casual. She settled for a pair of white wool pants and a white sweater with a huge rose knitted on the front.

The color matched the becoming flush in her cheeks. That and the feverish glitter in her eyes were the only outward signs of inner turmoil. Although her nerves were stretched to the breaking point, Christy forced herself to appear calm as she heard a car pull into the driveway.

Matt was using the company van again, since his car was still in the repair shop. He pulled up to the front door with a feeling of coming home.

Christy didn't rush out into the snow to greet him this time. She waited until he rang the bell. She had been wild with impatience before, but now that he was here, she felt shy and uncertain. Did Matt really mean what he said in the early-morning hours, or had it been too much to drink, as she suspected? Still, he was here. She opened the door.

"Hello, Christy." His muted voice sent vibrations through her.

She stared at him, unable to think of anything to say. What occurred to her was ridiculous. "You should have worn a heavier coat." He had on a zippered leather jacket over charcoal slacks.

Matt threw back his head and laughed. "You sound just like your aunt."

Christy smiled nervously. "I suppose a lot of her has rubbed off on me through the years." When Matt came inside and closed the door, she backed away. "It snowed again this morning. Were the roads clear?"

"Reasonably so." Like a jungle cat stalking its prey, he followed her over to the fireplace. His glowing eyes added to the impression.

"Did…would you like something to eat?" she asked.

"No, thanks. I had something before I left."

"A cup of coffee then? Aunt Sarah made pecan rolls."

Matt shook his head, glancing around. "Where is Aunt Sarah? I want to say happy New Year."

"She stayed at her friend Rhoda's last night. They had a ladies' bridge party."

"So *that's* why nobody answered!" Matt exclaimed. "I was about to call the Pine Grove police."

"It was New Year's Eve," Christy pointed out. "I don't imagine *you* were sitting at home."

"No, I was having a lousy time worrying about you."

"I can't imagine why."

"Because I'm an idiot," he said somberly.

"You didn't know I went to Squaw Valley, so you couldn't have been worried about an accident," she said slowly.

"It doesn't matter now." He looked uncomfortable.

Christy frowned. She had never seen Matt's poise ruffled before. "What were you worried about?"

"I should have known better! But all kinds of crazy things pop into a man's mind when there's no answer all night long."

She looked at him incredulously. "You thought I wasn't coming home? That I was spending the night with someone?"

He caught her face between his palms, tangling his fingers fiercely in her hair. "I would have strangled him with my bare hands!"

As Christy stared up into his intent face, a sense of power flooded through her. Her smile had the wisdom of Mona Lisa's. "Oh, Matt, you really *are* an idiot."

"I know," he groaned, sweeping her into his arms. "I wouldn't blame you if you sent me packing after the way I've treated you."

She smoothed the lines in his forehead. "It hasn't been fun," she admitted. "Why did you act like it was goodbye every time you left?"

He swung her into his arms and carried her over to the couch. Pillowing her head against his shoulder, he gazed down at her tenderly. "I've never been in love before, so I didn't recognize the symptoms."

"It's rarely fatal," she teased.

"You sound like an authority. How often have *you* been in love?" His tone was joking, but there was an underlying intensity.

"Never before." She traced the line of his high cheekbone under the smooth skin.

"Does that mean..." He couldn't finish the question.

"I've been in love with you since I opened the door on Christmas Eve and found you shivering on the doorstep," she said simply. "Maybe I didn't know it at that exact moment, but I found out a lot sooner than you did."

"My darling angel!" His kiss held both passion and tenderness. It was a total commitment. "I didn't realize. I thought you—"

Christy's blue eyes sparkled with mischief as she finished the sentence for him. "Just wanted your fantastic body?"

Matt smile ruefully. "It crossed my mind."

"You weren't wrong," she said softly.

He looked at her searchingly. "Is that all, Christy?"

She put her arms around his neck and gazed at him fondly. "Don't you listen to anything I say?"

"You've been so sheltered." He continued to look troubled. "It would be so easy for you to confuse desire with love."

Christy's arms tightened. "Oh no you don't, Matt Destry! I'm not going to let you talk yourself into another disappearing act."

"Never again, sweetheart!" he declared fervently. "I couldn't leave you now if I tried." His long fingers combed through her hair as he looked at her with deep emotion.

"Promise?" There was a trace of fear in the query that was meant to sound playful. Christy still found it hard to believe.

"Does this answer your question?"

Matt's mouth closed over hers for a kiss that was sweetly gentle. It expressed all the love and longing he'd tried vainly to deny. It was a sweetheart's kiss, a pledge of love.

Christy's fingertips traced his features. She needed to touch him, to be sure she wasn't dreaming. Her feathery caresses ranged over his closed eyelids, the straight bridge of his nose. She stroked the strong column of his neck, and then slid her hand inside the opening of his sport shirt.

When her nails raked lightly through the mat of dark hair on his broad chest, Matt made a sound deep in his throat. His arms tightened and his mouth became more urgent against hers. A familiar ache began to build inside Christy as he parted her lips for an arousing kiss. She felt the same mounting excitement Matt always brought just by being near.

He was charged with the same emotion. His hands roamed restlessly over her back, down to her waist. He caressed the strip of soft skin exposed by her hiked-up sweater. Then one hand moved underneath the waistband, burning a path up Christy's midriff to her breast.

"I've dreamed about your beautiful body," he muttered against her parted lips. "You're absolute perfection."

When his fingertips slipped inside her bra to circle her taut nipple, Christy uttered a tiny sound.

"Do you like that, my darling?" he murmured. "I want to please you in every way."

"You always have," she whispered.

"Sweet, beautiful Christy!" He feathered her face with frantic kisses. "I'm going to fill you with such joy! You're going to belong to me completely."

Their eyes held as he stood up, holding her against his chest. She clasped her arms around his neck and buried her face in his broad shoulder. As he carried her down the hall to her bedroom, Matt's murmured words of love fueled the fire he had lit.

He stood her on her feet beside the bed then removed her sweater and bra. Christy trembled as he looked at her with blazing eyes. When he caressed her breasts lingeringly, she swayed toward him.

Matt took her in his arms and molded her body tightly against his hard frame. The awesome force of his desire dissolved all her inhibitions. She was the one who pulled his head down and parted his lips for a passionate kiss, demanding release from the sweet torture he was inflicting.

"Don't make me rush you, angel," he groaned. "I want it to be so good for you."

"It will be," she whispered as she tugged the shirt out of his slacks.

The feeling of his bare skin against her sensitized breasts made Christy's legs feel boneless. She clung to him as he unfastened her slacks. When they slipped to the floor, Matt lifted her onto the bed and knelt over her, sliding his fingertips inside the elastic of her lacy panties.

She twisted one leg over the other, feeling suddenly shy as he removed her last garment. She was completely nude under his burning eyes. Matt gently parted her legs, looking at her with such love that Christy's breath caught in her throat.

"Trust me, my darling." His husky voice was tender. "I'll be so very gentle with you." When he touched her, the last barrier toppled.

"Please, Matt," she begged. "I want you so!"

Her pleading words galvanized him. Matt left her for just a moment to fling off his clothes. He returned to clasp her against his hardened body. The sensation was electric. It was like nothing Christy could ever imagine. She strained against him, seeking the fulfillment she knew he could bring.

"You don't know what you're doing to me!" His hoarse voice held a note of desperation as he turned her on to her back and lowered his body to hers.

Christy was pierced by a molten sensation. When she tensed momentarily, Matt held her tightly.

"Let it happen, sweetheart," he murmured.

Her taut body relaxed in his arms. This was the man she loved. After a few moments, an aching throb filled her. Christy moved restlessly, surging against Matt in an attempt to put out the fire that was consuming her. When his own movements were restrained, she arched her body against his, forcing a response.

Matt answered her need with a driving force that was deeply satisfying. It carried her higher and higher. She was filled with ecstasy, trembling on the brink of an unknown, but glorious experience. Suddenly a molten wave engulfed her rigid body. Christy was catapulted into space, flooded with rapture so intense that she clung to Matt for protection.

He cradled her in his arms and guided her back to earth. The passion that had racked her dissipated slowly as she floated down safely in his embrace.

They remained intertwined for a long time. Finally Matt stirred. He kissed her closed eyelids tenderly. "Was it what you hoped for, sweetheart?" he murmured.

"It was so much more." She lifted her face for a kiss that was sweet with satisfied completion. "I didn't know it would be like this."

"It's going to be even better." His hand moved slowly over her body. "I'm going to make love to you every night. I'm going to satisfy you a hundred different ways."

Christy sighed happily at the delirious thought, even though she knew there were obstacles. "Are you planning to commute between here and San Francisco?" she teased.

He nibbled on her earlobe. "No, I'm planning on prying you out of Pine Grove."

She gave him a startled look. "What do you mean?"

"I want you in my bed every night." His eyes smoldered with awakening desire. "I want to hold you in my arms in the darkness, and see your beautiful face when I wake up every morning."

"Are you asking me to move in with you?" Christy asked slowly.

Matt smiled. "It sure beats commuting."

The idea was so foreign that she was speechless. Her conventional upbringing had always taught that girls didn't live with a man, even if they were planning on getting married. But times had changed. Matt's caressing hand on her bare body told Christy how much! Still, could she live with him openly?

Matt's expression was tender as he gazed at her sober face. "I know the idea is frightening, honey, but we'll be together. I'll see that you're happy."

Christy knew what her answer would be when his lips touched hers. A piece of paper wouldn't make their love any more sacred. She already belonged to this man totally. As the idea took hold, Christy was filled with rising excitement.

"I want to make you happy too." She smoothed his ruffled hair lovingly. "I'll get a fantastic job and help with the rent."

Matt's expression was suddenly guarded. "You won't have to do that, sweetheart."

"I want to help, Matt. I know you're just getting started. And besides, don't couples share everything equally in a modern relationship?" she asked earnestly.

He stared at her incredulously. "You think I want—" He stopped short, and then started again slowly. "I think you're confused about the sort of relationship I had in mind."

"No, I understand." Her clear blue eyes met his trustingly. "You've always been honest with me. It's the thing I respect most about you. We won't ever have to play games with each other."

Matt was appalled. He was so sure Christy knew he was asking her to marry him. Why hadn't he come right out with a proposal instead of letting her commit herself? Matt was touched that she had agreed to live with him, knowing what a difficult decision it must have been. But now she might think he'd been testing her, finding out if she loved him for himself instead of his money. Everything he'd done up to this point would seem to indicate as much. Would she understand how it had happened and forgive him?

Matt sighed. "We have to have a talk, angel." When Christy snuggled up against him, lifting her beautiful face, his body quickened. "It can wait," he muttered hoarsely.

Chapter Five

Matt never did get around to having a talk with Christy. Nothing was as important as holding her in his arms and repeating his vow of love endlessly. When their precious time together ran out and he had to leave, Matt eased his conscience by promising himself he'd straighten everything out on Saturday. It was only two days away.

On Friday Christy received the bogus letter informing her that she'd won a cruise. Her initial reaction was astounded joy. Then she thought about Matt and their new relationship. They hadn't had a chance to discuss when she'd be joining him in San Francisco, but it would be soon. Did she want to leave him for two weeks at the very beginning? It would be wonderful if Matt could go with her, but that was out of the question. He had just started a new job.

"This is what you've always dreamed of, child." Sarah couldn't understand Christy's curious reluctance to claim her prize. "It's lucky you don't have to be at work until Monday. You can use this time to drive to San Francisco and make the arrangements."

"There's no big hurry."

Christy had put off telling Sarah about Matt and their plans. It wasn't going to be easy. Although her aunt wouldn't try to stop her, Christy knew the older woman wouldn't be happy about the idea. It was probably cowardly, but Christy had decided to wait until Matt was with her before she broke the news.

"I don't understand you," Sarah scolded. "What are you waiting for?"

"Well, I have to get time off from my job, and...and buy some new clothes. I need a bathing suit," she finished lamely.

"You won't find any in Pine Grove at this time of year. You can go shopping when you're in San Francisco finding out when the next cruise is. For all you know, it might not be for a month yet. How are you going to ask for time off from work if you don't know when you want it?"

"That's true." Christy let herself be persuaded. "I guess it wouldn't hurt to pay a visit to the steamship line." The deciding factor was that she could also see Matt and start making plans.

Christy remembered the name of Matt's company from seeing it on the side of the van. She looked up the address in a phone book when she got to the city.

The Transamerica pyramid was one of the most prestigious office buildings in downtown San Francisco. Christy was suitably impressed when she discovered the corporate headquarters of Matt's new company occupied a whole floor near the top.

The reception room was furnished in tranquil beiges, with excellent prints on the cream-colored walls. Christy's footsteps were muffled by thick carpeting as she walked toward the receptionist's desk.

An attractive young woman greeted her with a smile. "Can I help you?"

"Yes, I'm looking for someone in the engineering department—a man named Matt Destry. He's a new employee here," Christy added helpfully.

The woman's smile faded. "Is this some kind of joke?"

Christy looked at her uncertainly. "I don't understand."

"Neither do I. Who did you want to see? Mr. Destry, or someone in engineering?"

Christy had a sense of foreboding. Had Matt lied to her about the job he held? Didn't he know it wouldn't matter to her if he were the janitor? She was tempted to leave before he found out she had discovered his secret. But Christy knew she mustn't let a lie develop between them.

"Matt said . . . that is . . . You *do* have a Mr. Destry working here?"

"Perhaps I'd better let you talk to his secretary," the receptionist said, looking at her cautiously. "It's the office at the end of the hall."

Christy followed the instructions automatically, although she felt slightly dazed. Hadn't she made herself clear? Surely Matt would have told her if he had a position grand enough for a secretary.

Another attractive woman greeted her in an office even more opulent that the waiting room. She also smiled and asked how she could help.

"I'm looking for Matt Destry," Christy said hesitantly.

"Do you have an appointment?"

"No, I . . . I just stopped by to talk to him."

"I'm sorry, but Mr. Destry only sees people by appointment."

Christy's feeling of unreality deepened. It was all very strange. Could there be two Matt Destrys? It wasn't very probable. Yet what other explanation was there? As she was staring at the other woman, wondering what to do, Matt came out of the inner office.

He was thumbing rapidly through the papers he held in one hand. "Linda, this report has to go to Newcombe as soon as—" The words broke off abruptly as he looked up and saw Christy. Matt's first expression was one of pleasure. "Christy! What are you doing here?"

"I came to see you, but no one would tell me where you worked."

Consternation replaced his joy. "Oh, God, I didn't want you to find out like this!"

"What is it, Matt? What are you keeping from me?"

"Come inside," he said gently, taking her arm and leading her toward the other room.

Christy looked around in disbelief at the comfortable leather couch and chairs, the paintings on the paneled walls. "What are we doing here? Whose office is this?"

"Sit down, darling. I have to talk to you."

Christy allowed Matt to guide her to the couch, although she had an overwhelming impulse to turn and run. Something was terribly wrong, and suddenly she didn't want to know what it was.

"Couldn't it wait until you come to Pine Grove tomorrow?" she asked haltingly.

"No, it's something I should have told you long ago. I did try several times, but it always ended in a misunderstanding. I never meant to deceive you, Christy." His face held deep regret.

The bottom was dropping out of Christy's world, and she had a glimmering of the reason. "What are you trying to say, Matt, that you're married?"

"Good Lord, no! Whatever gave you that idea?" He took both her hands. "I guess I'd better start at the beginning, which would be Christmas Eve."

"Don't drag it out, Matt! What does that have to do with all this?" Christy waved at the luxurious office.

"Hear me out, honey. It's all part of it. I was cold and hungry that night. You took me in a gave me the guest room. I couldn't believe it."

"You didn't have anyplace to stay," she said simply.

"Well, actually, I'd reserved a hotel room in Squaw Valley."

"You didn't tell us that!"

"I never had a chance. You and your aunt assumed I was a homeless drifter. Every time I tried to correct the misconception, you thought I was just saving face. At first it amused me. Then when you took me in without question, I was astonished. I'd never known such kind people."

Christy was having difficulty understanding any of it. "What were you doing in Pine Grove in the first place?"

"I was on my way to the ski lodge when my car was forced off the road and wrecked. I was looking for a phone, and yours was the closest house to the highway."

"But why did you stay?" she asked helplessly.

"Partly because the emergency service wouldn't tow me until the day after Christmas." His thumb moved slowly over the soft skin of her wrist. "But mostly because I met the most exquisite girl in the world, and I wanted to know her better."

Christy scarcely heard him. "You weren't out of a job either, were you?"

"No," he answered quietly.

She looked at him searchingly, noticing for the first time the elegantly tailored dark suit and handsome tie. He seemed like a complete stranger. "Who are you really, Matt?"

"I'm the same man I was before, honey. The rest is just window dressing."

Christy glanced around the spacious room. "This is your office, isn't it?"

Matt nodded.

"I don't suppose you're an engineer. What position do you hold here?"

"I really am an engineer, but I...also own CompuTrend."

She stared at him in shocked amazement. "The whole company?"

"Yes."

Christy felt as though she'd stumbled into a hall of crazed mirrors. Her whole world was distorted. The man she loved had made a fool of her! It was just starting to sink in.

"You lied to me!" She jerked her hands away and sprang to her feet.

"Be fair, Christy," Matt pleaded. "I never told you anything that was untrue."

"You knew exactly what you were doing," she stormed. "You accepted our hospitality under false pretenses. Our homespun Christmas must have made a hilarious story to tell your sophisticated friends. Is that why you came back, to get more material to amuse them with?" Her slim body was as taut as a violin string. "I hope you included that touching moment in the barn when I threw myself at you.''

''Christy, darling, how can you even think—''

''It was too easy to take me then, wasn't it? I wasn't any challenge. The only way to make it fun was to build up to the big seduction act.''

Matt's fingers bit into her rigid shoulders. ''Stop it!'' he commanded. ''You know there isn't a word of truth in any of that.''

''I suppose you really meant it when you said you loved me,'' she said scornfully.

''Didn't yesterday tell you anything?'' he demanded.

''You have a knack for not answering awkward questions,'' she said sardonically. ''But I finally get the message. You never intended to return on Saturday, did you? The charade was played out. If I hadn't come here today, I'd never have seen you again.''

He looked at her incredulously. ''How about the plans we made?''

''That must really have amused you—my offer to pay half the rent.'' Her laughter had a ragged sound. ''If your apartment's anything like this office, you need a roommate with a better job than I could get.''

''I never expected you to be my roommate, *or* pay for anything.''

''That's what I just said.'' Christy swallowed hard to hold back the tears that clogged her throat. At least she wouldn't give him that satisfaction. ''Goodbye, Matt. It's been—educational.''

''You don't mean that, angel.'' He tried to draw her close, but she held him off with her hands on his forearms. ''I'm sorry for not leveling with you in the be-

ginning, but I never meant to hurt you. At least grant
me that much.''

"Conscience, Matt?'' She managed a ghost of a
smile. "Well, maybe there's hope for you yet.'' She
twisted out of his grasp and started for the door, pass-
ing his secretary in the entrance.

"Your three o'clock appointment is in the waiting
room, Mr. Destry,'' Linda said discreetly.

"Christy, wait!'' Matt called over her shoulder. He
put Linda aside, but the momentary delay enabled
Christy to get away.

She ran down the hall, heedless of curious looks. Her
one goal was to escape further humiliation. A waiting
elevator was like a gift from heaven. Christy pushed the
lobby button with a shaking finger.

At first she hurried down the block, dodging around
slow-moving window-shoppers to gain distance in case
Matt tried to follow her. Although it was scarcely likely,
Christy thought bitterly. He'd had the grace to be
ashamed of himself at the end. Misery washed over her
in waves. How could she have misjudged Matt so? How
could he have been so deliberately cruel?

She should have known he was hiding something
when he avoided talking about himself. He had even
told her she was too trusting. Well, never again! She'd
learned a bitter lesson. Men would do anything to get
what they wanted.

Matt had her staked out as prey from the moment she
opened the door on Christmas Eve. Christy shivered,
remembering the appreciative glimmer in his dark eyes
when he saw her. He was like a hungry wolf sighting a
helpless lamb.

Christy burned with indignation when she thought
about how cunning he'd been, playing on her inexperi-

ence until *she* was the one who begged *him* to make love to her! But the truly unforgivable thing was letting her think he wanted to make it a permanent relationship.

After seeing Matt in his own environment, Christy knew he hadn't been serious. The idea that she would fit into his sophisticated life-style was laughable. She would be an embarrassment. Matt had practically admitted it in one unguarded moment. Christy suddenly remembered the strange look on his face when he said she'd misunderstood the kind of arrangement he had in mind. It was all pillow talk. She was supposed to go along with it, but not expect it to happen.

As Christy's footsteps dragged, she forced herself to stop dwelling on the past and face the future. What was she going to do now? All her plans had centered around Matt. He'd been the focal point of her life. It was folly to depend on another person to that extent, but the hurt was too new. She needed time to pull herself together, to get away alone until she was able to accept the fact that she'd made a terrible mistake.

Suddenly Christy recalled her sweepstakes prize, the reason she'd come to the city. It was at least a temporary answer. Her aimless steps quickened as she headed for the steamship office.

"When is your next cruise to the Caribbean on the *Sun Queen*?" she asked a reservation clerk a short time later.

"We have a sailing tomorrow," the young woman informed her.

"Great, I'll take it!" Christy exclaimed. It was the one ray of sunshine in a gray world.

"I'm afraid that isn't possible. We're sold out. I guess everyone wants to get away from the rain and fog this time of year, but we have another ship going out in six weeks.''

"I can't wait that long! I won this contest, and they told me I could claim my prize whenever I wanted." Christy pulled the letter out of her purse.

The woman examined it with interest. "Well, lucky you, Miss Blake! The only problem is that we're filled to capacity, as I told you. I can book you on the next cruise, though."

"Don't you have anything at all?" Christy asked hopelessly.

"Let me double-check." After punching some keys on a computer, the reservation clerk viewed the small screen regretfully. "I'm really sorry. All we have is a tiny, inside cubbyhole that you wouldn't be interested in." She brightened momentarily. "We do have a cancellation on the Antigua suite. It's really elegant. You can have that if you pay the difference."

"How much would it be?" Christy asked. She blanched at the price quoted. It was completely out of the question. She couldn't wait six weeks, though. After a brief moment, Christy made up her mind. "I'll take the small cabin."

"But you're entitled to a deluxe one," the woman objected. "I don't think we can refund the difference."

"It doesn't matter. Just make out my ticket."

Sarah was waiting expectantly when Christy got home. "Did you make the arrangements?"

"I leave tomorrow," Christy said grimly.

"Tomorrow! That's what I call fast work." The older woman frowned. "You don't seem too excited about it."

"How can you say that?" Christy tried to appear animated. "I'm positively ecstatic."

"What's wrong, Christy?" Sarah asked quietly.

"I don't know what you're talking about. Everything's just peachy." She gathered her things, averting her face. "I have a big day tomorrow, so I'd better get some sleep."

"Matt has been calling every fifteen minutes. He wouldn't tell me what happened either. Did you two have an argument?"

Christy gathered her strength for a denial, but she couldn't go through with it. She had never lied to her aunt. "Oh, Aunt Sarah, what am I going to do?"

Sarah drew Christy into her arms and let her cry out all her grief. When the storm was over, Christy told her the whole story.

"None of this sounds like Matt," Sarah said slowly. "I'll admit it's a shock, but are you sure you didn't jump to conclusions about his motives?"

"His only excuse was that he never meant to hurt me," Christy said drearily.

"I can't believe I could be that wrong about a person." Sarah's face was troubled.

"We live in a different world. We haven't had any experience with men like Matt."

"Maybe." Sarah was unconvinced. "I'd still like to talk to him."

"Please don't," Christy begged. "Just chalk it up to experience. That's what I've done. By the time I get back from this cruise I'll have forgotten all about him."

Sarah's face was inscrutable. "That's the right idea, child. Go to bed and get some rest."

When the telephone rang, Christy looked panicky. "If that's for me, I don't want to talk to anyone!"

"Don't worry, I'll take care of it," Sarah soothed.

The phone call was evidently for her aunt, because Christy heard the murmur of her voice for a long time.

Sarah helped Christy pack the next morning, ignoring her lack of enthusiasm. Sarah was the one who insisted on including lacy underwear and evening clothes.

"I'm really going for a change of scenery," Christy protested. "The last thing I need is another romantic entanglement."

"It never hurts to be prepared," Sarah answered serenely. "Suppose you met a prince who was incognito?"

Christy smiled, one of her first natural reactions. "I'd probably tell him to buzz off, and get in trouble with the State Department for insulting a friendly nation."

"Well, try not to start World War Three," Sarah observed dryly. "You'd never forgive yourself."

Her aunt drove Christy to the ship but declined to go aboard. Christy clung to her for a long moment.

"I wish you were coming with me, Aunt Sarah."

"I imagine you'll have a better time without me. Don't dawdle, child. I have to get back to the ranch." The gentle expression on Sarah's face belied her impatient tone.

Christy walked slowly up the gangplank after her aunt had driven away, the only passenger without a smile of anticipation. She waited her turn listlessly at the purser's desk.

He greeted her with professional heartiness and located her name on a typewritten list. "Welcome aboard, Miss Blake. The steward will show you to your cabin."

Christy followed the uniformed steward into an elevator that rose several floors. She trailed after him down a long corridor to her designated cabin. But when he opened the door, Christy knew there had been a mistake. It was a luxurious suite.

The living room had a couch, several chairs and assorted tables. Opening off it was a bedroom with a king-size bed. Wide glass windows provided a stunning view of the ocean beyond a private lanai furnished with deck chairs.

"There's been a mistake," Christy said regretfully. "This isn't my cabin."

The steward referred to a slip of paper in his hand. "Miss Blake, Antigua suite."

"No, it was offered to me, but I couldn't afford it," she explained. "There must have been a mix-up."

"Why don't you wait here while I find out about it," the man advised.

Christy felt the engines start as she moved over to the window to look out at the Golden Gate Bridge. It would be lovely to occupy this luxurious cabin, but it was just one more thing she couldn't have. The ship gathered speed, and tiny ripples turned into white-capped waves.

"I took the small closet and left the large one for you," a deep, familiar voice remarked from behind her.

Christy was sure she was hearing things. She whirled to look disbelievingly at Matt. It couldn't be! She had to be imagining him, but he looked too vitally alive to be a mirage.

"What are you doing here?" she whispered.

Matt smiled, as though it was the most natural thing in the world. "Aunt Sarah thought you might be lonely, so she suggested I join you."

"She would never do a thing like that!"

Matt's smile turned into a grin that showed white teeth in his deeply tanned face. "Well she *does* expect me to marry you."

"How could you let her believe such a thing?" Christy's cheeks were pink with outrage. "This is even worse than all the other rotten tricks you've pulled! Haven't you done enough already? Did you have to destroy her faith completely? You are the most—"

Matt didn't seem the least bit disturbed by Christy's tirade. He closed the distance between them while she was ranting and took her in his arms. She struggled wildly, still sputtering angry words, but Matt's mouth effectively stopped them.

Christy was no match for his strength. His fingers anchored her long hair, holding her for a penetrating kiss that made shivers race up her spine, even in her outraged state. She was powerless to stop him when he molded her body so closely that she could feel every muscle in his hard thighs. Her struggles only made the contact more inflaming.

Gradually, a creeping warmth made her efforts less frantic. Christy's clutching fingers relaxed, and her hands moved tentatively over Matt's broad shoulders. Her mind protested that it was madness, but her body's response was more imperative. His mouth was irresistible, and his slow caresses overcame all objections.

When she stopped fighting him, Matt swung her into his arms and carried her into the bedroom. Christy burried her face in his neck, clinging to him tightly. It was insane to let him use her again, but she had no choice.

Matt joined her on the wide bed without letting her out of his arms. His dark head was poised over hers.

"At least I've learned how to end an argument with you." He smiled mischievously.

She turned her head away, unable to look at him. "You don't fight fair," she muttered.

"You know that line about love and war."

His long fingers unfastened the top button of her blouse, and then the next one. Christy made a feeble motion to stop him, then dropped her hand. How could she deny her own longing when his mouth was leaving a trail of stinging little kisses on her sensitive skin? After her blouse was open to the waist, he unclasped her bra and smoothed it away from her breasts. Christy trembled as he bent his head to kiss each rosy peak.

"My beautiful love," he murmured. "Do you think I'd ever let you get away?"

A storm gathered inside Christy as he undressed her completely. It built in intensity as he caressed every secret part of her. When she was nude beneath his glowing eyes, Matt trailed his fingertips down the length of her body.

"How did I ever deserve such a gift?" His voice was husky. "You gave yourself to me, and now you're mine forever. I'll never let you go."

"Oh, Matt, Matt." Christy reached out for him blindly.

His face revealed naked emotion. "You don't know what it does to me when you call my name! I want to hear it on your lips when I bring you the greatest joy."

He left her briefly to fling off his clothes in a blur of movement, then returned to clasp her in his arms.

"Love me, darling," he murmured deeply.

"I do," she whispered in total surrender.

Matt moved her body tenderly under his. He kissed her gently at first, and then more urgently as she responded with unashamed passion. When Christy murmured in his ear, Matt's arms tightened convulsively.

Their need for each other was so great that the storm was brief, but totally satisfying. Afterward, Christy lay quietly with her cheek on Matt's bare chest, listening to his heart return to a slower beat. His caressing hand on her body was the final, perfect touch.

Neither stirred for a long time. Finally Matt said, "I arranged with the captain to marry us, but not until tomorrow. I hope you don't mind."

Christy drew back to look at him with incredulous hope. "You really mean it?"

Matt chuckled as he stared pointedly at her nude body. "Don't you think it's indicated? What would Aunt Sarah say if I didn't marry you?"

"You mean it's all a joke," she said dully.

Christy was filled with desolation. Once more she had let Matt raise her hopes. When would she ever learn?

Matt's expression changed as he saw the light go out of her eyes. He pulled her back in his arms and stroked her hair tenderly.

"Do you think after we're married for forty or fifty years you might start to trust me?" he asked gently. "I love you more than I ever thought it was possible for a man to love a woman. I want to marry you and live with you for the rest of our lives. Does that answer your question?"

Christy flung her arms around his neck and rained frantic kisses over his face. "Oh, Matt, you don't know what I went through when I thought I'd never see you again!"

"Silly little Christy," he said fondly. "You don't know much about men—and now you've lost your chance to learn." His eyes darkened with renewed passion. "From now on, I'm the only man in your life."

"I never wanted any other," she whispered.

He parted her lips for a kiss so blissful that Christy was sure this was what heaven must be like.

"I hear bells," she said dreamily.

Matt chuckled. "That's the dinner gong."

"I'm not hungry," she said softly.

"Neither am I," he murmured against her mouth. After a long moment he raised his head slightly. "We're probably at the captain's table."

Christy's lips slid along Matt's strong jawline. "Do you think he'd mind if we were late?"

"I think he'd understand." Matt's voice held a special note as he gazed deeply into her eyes.

*   *   *   *   *